"Thank you for not leaving me alone."

He reached across the table and his big hand engulfed hers, warming some of the cold spots she'd had inside. "There's no way I'd leave you alone, Lexie. I know what it's like to be alone with grief and I don't want that for you."

As she looked into his soft gray eyes, she wanted him. She wanted the warmth of his body wrapped around hers. She needed him to keep the horror at bay.

"Come to bed with me, Nick. Come to bed and make love to me."

His eyes flared wide at her words. "Lexie, that's probably not a good idea tonight. You're grieving and you aren't thinking straight and the last thing I'd want to do is take advantage of you."

"You wouldn't be. I know you've already had your Cupid arrow, Nick. This isn't about love, it's about need." She got up from the table. "I need to be held. I need to feel alive. I need you, Nick."

CARLA CASSIDY

SCENE OF THE CRIME: WIDOW CREEK

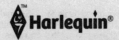

TORONTO NEW YORK LONDON
AMSTERDAM PARIS SYDNEY HAMBURG
STOCKHOLM ATHENS TOKYO MILAN MADRID
PRAGUE WARSAW BUDAPEST AUCKLAND

To Valerie Francis

For Sundays and girl talk and all your support! For laughter and jewelry and a little touch of sanity in my life. All I can say is thanks!

Recycling programs
for this product may
not exist in your area.

ISBN-13: 978-0-373-69568-3

SCENE OF THE CRIME: WIDOW CREEK

ABOUT THE AUTHOR

Carla Cassidy is an award-winning author who has written more than fifty novels for Harlequin Books. In 1995, she won Best Silhouette Romance from *RT Book Reviews* for *Anything for Danny*. In 1998, she also won a Career Achievement Award for Best Innovative Series from *RT Book Reviews*.

Carla believes the only thing better than curling up with a good book to read is sitting down at the computer with a good story to write. She's looking forward to writing many more books and bringing hours of pleasure to readers.

Books by Carla Cassidy

HARLEQUIN INTRIGUE
1077—THE SHERIFF'S SECRETARY
1114—PROFILE DURANGO
1134—INTERROGATING THE BRIDE*
1140—HEIRESS RECON*
1146—PREGNESIA*
1175—SCENE OF THE CRIME: BRIDGEWATER, TEXAS
1199—ENIGMA
1221—WANTED: BODYGUARD
1258—SCENE OF THE CRIME: BACHELOR MOON
1287—BY ORDER OF THE PRINCE
1301—SCENE OF THE CRIME: WIDOW CREEK

*The Recovery Men

Don't miss any of our special offers. Write to us at the following address for information on our newest releases.

Harlequin Reader Service
U.S.: 3010 Walden Ave., P.O. Box 1325, Buffalo, NY 14269
Canadian: P.O. Box 609, Fort Erie, Ont. L2A 5X3

CAST OF CHARACTERS

Lexie Forbes—She'd come to Widow Creek seeking her missing twin sister but instead had found danger...and more.

Nick Walker—Was he friend or foe to Lexie?

Lana Forbes—Lexie's missing twin. Had she walked away from her life or stumbled onto something malevolent in the small town?

Gary Wendell—Was the chief of police a good guy or somebody who would do anything to protect the secrets of his town?

Bo Richards—A handsome rancher who dated Lana. Was he the last person to see her alive? And was he responsible for her death?

Clay Cole—A tough guy with an attitude. What did he know, if anything, about what had happened to Lana?

Chapter One

Lexie Forbes rarely left her job at the Kansas City FBI field office early, but on this Friday afternoon she knocked off work at three and headed toward her car in the parking lot. There was nothing pressing on her desk, just the usual cons and perverts for her to chase down. But she'd awakened that morning with a vague sense of anxiety that she hadn't quite been able to shake off.

She knew the source of the anxiety—her twin sister, Lauren. They were extremely close and spoke on the phone to each other at least once or twice a day, but for the past two days Lexie had been unable to get hold of her sister.

As she walked through the parking lot, the first fallen autumn leaves swirled around her feet and a cool breeze danced unexpected goose bumps along her arms.

She reached her car, unlocked it and then slid in behind the wheel. She'd just put the key in and started the engine when it struck, an excruciating pain that slammed into the back of her head with such force it momentarily stole her breath away.

It was there only a moment and then gone, leaving

her gasping for air and holding on to the steering wheel with clenched fingers.

"Whoa," she finally breathed. What was that all about? It had felt like a bomb had detonated in the base of her brain. With a shaky hand she reached up and adjusted the rearview mirror so she could look at her reflection.

She wasn't sure what she expected to see, but the woman who stared back at her looked the same as always. Short, light brown, spiked hair with a vivid pink streak, black-rimmed glasses nearly hiding green eyes and no blood or missing skull from that sharp pain.

Adjusting the mirror back where it belonged, her thoughts once again shot to her sister and the anxiety swelled bigger and tighter in her chest. There had been a time several years ago when Lexie had suffered from inexplicable arm pain for a couple of hours. Later she'd discovered that Lauren had broken her arm. It had been one of those crazy twin things that nobody understood and that only happened occasionally.

Had Lauren hit her head? Had Lexie just experienced her twin's pain? She dismissed the idea. Each and every pain Lexie suffered wasn't tied to her twin sister.

As she pulled out of the parking lot she decided that if she didn't get hold of Lauren when she got to her apartment, then a road trip was definitely in order.

Four months ago Lauren had realized her dream and bought six acres of land in a small town about an hour and a half from the Kansas City area. Over the last couple of years she'd become an established dog breeder and trainer and had wanted enough property to expand her business.

Lexie had helped her move but hadn't been back to visit since that time. It was definitely past time for a trip to see her sister. She had the weekend open and this was a perfect opportunity for a surprise visit.

Once Lexie got home to her small apartment she tried her sister again, both on her landline and on her cell phone. When she still didn't get an answer she packed a bag, locked the apartment door and headed toward the small Kansas town of Widow Creek.

It was a pleasant drive. Traffic was light, and once she left the city she enjoyed the country scenery. Her favorite oldies played on the radio and she sang along until she reached the city limits of the small town.

It was just after five when she pulled up in front of her sister's place. The ranch-style farmhouse looked warm and inviting with pots of colorful flowers and a wicker rocking chair on the porch.

She got out of the car and gazed around. She'd forgotten that the place was a bit isolated, with only one other house visible in the distance. Aware of the sound of barking dogs, she walked to the side of the house where a large fenced area contained four young German shepherds.

They all raced to the fence with youthful pup eagerness, stepping on each other in an effort to get closer to her. She might have laughed at their antics if she didn't see that their food and water bowls were empty.

Lauren would never allow any of her dogs to go

without food and water. The disquiet that had simmered inside her for the past two days now roared into full-bloom alarm.

She left the dog pen and hurried to the front door where she knocked. "Lauren? Lauren, are you in there? It's me." She waited only a moment and when no answer came she pulled out her keys and used the one that Lauren had given her on moving day.

Visions of her sister filled her head. Maybe she'd slipped in the shower and hurt herself to the point she couldn't get to a phone. Or maybe she was in bed, deathly ill, and couldn't rouse herself enough to make a call for help.

She unlocked the door and then pulled her gun and held it steady in her hand as she shoved the door open with her foot. Even though Lexie's job with the FBI consisted of her sitting in a small cubicle in front of a computer, she'd been trained to be proficient with her weapon.

As she entered the small foyer the first thing she noticed was that the house smelled slightly musty, as if it had been closed up for too long.

There was a low woof and Zeus greeted her. The old German shepherd ran to her like she was his new best friend. He sat on the floor at her feet and released a low, mournful whine.

Lexie dropped her gun back into her purse. There was no way anybody threatening could be in the house without Zeus letting her know.

"Hey, boy." She crouched down and scrubbed the dog behind his ears. "Hey, buddy, where's your mama?"

Zeus closed his eyes and released what sounded like a contented sigh as she continued to scratch behind his ears. She finally stood up and walked into the kitchen, then worried all over again when she saw that Zeus's food and water bowls were also empty.

She checked the rest of the house and confirmed that nobody was home, then returned to the kitchen and got food and water for Zeus. He attacked the food as if he were starving.

As Lexie watched him eat, her heart beat a rhythm of dread. What was going on here? Where was Lauren? Her dogs were her family and there was no way she'd leave them like this.

When she'd walked through the house she'd seen nothing amiss, no sign of trouble. The rooms were all neat and tidy, just the way Lauren always kept them.

The last time she'd talked to her sister had been Tuesday evening and Lauren hadn't mentioned going anywhere. Lauren almost never traveled because she didn't like leaving the care of the dogs to anyone else.

As Zeus finished his meal, Lexie stared out the back window where there were several outbuildings and beyond them an expanse of thick woods.

Was Lauren out there somewhere? Had she taken a walk, somehow fallen and hurt herself and been unable to summon help? She grabbed the leash that hung on a hook by the back door and then called to Zeus.

If Lauren was out there somewhere surely Zeus

would find her. Lauren had gotten the dog when he was eight weeks old and he was now nine. No matter how many other dogs passed through Lauren's life, she and Zeus had always had a special bond.

Moments later, with Zeus on the leash, Lexie stepped out the back door and headed toward the outbuildings. Zeus bounded ahead on the length of leash she gave him as she tried to tamp down the overwhelming sense of dread that grew stronger with each minute that passed.

Her dread increased as she opened the door of the detached garage and found Lauren's truck inside. Where could she be without her vehicle?

Next she checked the first large shed, which held a variety of items Lauren used for her various training sessions. There were poles and jumps, risers and items used for agility training. Unfortunately, there was no Lauren.

She moved to the second, smaller shed and discovered it held only gardening tools. She told herself not to jump to any conclusions, but it was hard not to with the knot of fear that pressed tight in her chest.

The woods. It was the only place she had left to check. She looked at her watch. Almost six. She'd maybe get two good hours in before darkness began to fall and made a search impossible.

She took off with Zeus in tow and within minutes was surrounded by tall trees and thick brush. "Lauren!" she called every few steps and then stopped and listened for any kind of answering reply. But there was nothing except the sound of Zeus crunching leaves beneath his big paws.

"Zeus, find your mommy," she commanded the dog.

He barked and danced in place, as if unsure what she wanted from him. They walked for what seemed like an eternity until she finally reached a rocky creek bed with just a trickle of water running in it. She sank down on the edge, Zeus at her side and looked around with a sense of failure as she rested.

Darkness was slamming down with a swiftness that was disheartening. She'd done a cursory check of all the property and Zeus had never given an indication that his master might be near.

"Where are you, Lauren?" She had a bad feeling. None of this was right and she couldn't imagine any scenario that would allow any of this to make sense.

Lauren was definitely not the type to just take off somewhere with no thought to her dogs, no thought for Lexie. Something was terribly wrong.

She pulled herself up from the creek bank and headed back to the house. Maybe by now Lauren had returned. Or perhaps a friend had picked her up for shopping or dinner out and they hadn't returned yet. Of course that wouldn't explain why she hadn't answered Lexie's phone calls since Tuesday night.

The shadows of night had begun to cling to the house as Lexie reentered through the back door. For the first time in her life she hated to see nightfall. She removed Zeus from the leash and then went into Lauren's bedroom and stood staring at the neatly made bed.

The room breathed the essence of Lauren. It was infused with warmth from the peach and navy ruffled bedspread to the photo of the two sisters hugging on the nightstand. A faint scent of the orange blossom lotion that Lauren loved lingered in the air, intensifying Lexie's overwhelming sense of confusion and worry.

She thought back to the last phone conversation she'd had with her sister but couldn't think of anything Lauren had said that might explain her absence here. Lauren had talked about the dogs, about how excited she was about the growth of her business, but she hadn't mentioned going anywhere for any extended period of time.

There was absolutely no reason to believe that she'd been missing since that phone conversation, Lexie told herself. She might have left the house that morning for some sort of day trip and hadn't realized the dogs were out of water.

The fact that the house smelled like it had been closed up for a couple of days didn't mean anything either. Maybe she was only thinking bad thoughts because of her job. As an FBI agent she was trained to look at the worst-case scenario.

An unmistakable sound came from behind her—the slide and click of a bullet being chambered in a shotgun. She froze as her heart nearly stopped beating.

"Who the hell are you and what are you doing in Lauren's bedroom?" The deep male voice was calm but held a steely edge.

She raised her hands above her head and slowly

turned. He stood in the threshold of the bedroom. With his dark hair and gunmetal gray eyes, he was a hot hunk in a pair of tight jeans and a navy pullover. And he had the business end of a shotgun pointed directly at her heart.

NICK WALKER SLOWLY LOWERED the shotgun as he recognized the woman standing before him as the same one in the picture with Lauren on the nightstand.

"You're Lexie," he said as some of the tension ebbed from him.

Even though she and Lauren were identical twins it was obvious Lexie had gone to some extremes to find her own identity. Lauren wore contacts while the woman standing before him wore oversized black-rimmed glasses that almost hid the beauty of her bright green eyes. Lauren's hair was shoulder-length and Lexie's was short and spiked and sporting an unexpected pink streak.

Nick was surprised to feel a small kick of attraction in the pit of his stomach, something he'd never felt for his friend and neighbor, Lauren.

"The real question is who in the hell are you and what are you doing in Lauren's bedroom?" she asked, her chin lifted and eyes narrowed.

"I'm Nick Walker and I live next door. Why don't we both get out of Lauren's bedroom and go into the kitchen where we can talk."

He didn't wait for her response but rather turned and left the bedroom. During the past four months he and

Lauren had become good friends and in that time she'd spoken often of her twin sister.

He knew that Lexie worked for the cybercrime unit with the FBI in Kansas City, that Lauren worried that Lexie had a better relationship with her computer than with any real people and that the twins had been raised by their father who had passed away five years ago.

He leaned his shotgun against the kitchen wall and then sat at the round oak table. She came into the kitchen holding a handgun and wearing a scowl.

"Now you can answer some more of my questions," she said as she eased down into the chair opposite him.

"There's no need for your gun," he replied easily. "I'm on your side."

"I don't know that yet," she countered. "What are you doing here and how did you get inside?"

"Lauren and I exchanged keys to our homes about a month after she moved in here. Since neither of us have family here, we thought it would be a good idea in case of emergency. I let myself in when I saw the unfamiliar car out front and I knew that Lauren wasn't home."

Lexie stared at him unblinking. Under normal circumstances the length of time of the eye contact would have bordered on inappropriate, but he told himself these weren't normal circumstances. "Where is she?" There was a faint whisper of fear in her voice.

"I don't know. I haven't seen her since Tuesday. She's been working with my dog and I came here late afternoon on Wednesday for my usual session and she wasn't here."

He tried not to notice the scent of her, a clean fresh smell coupled with a hint of sweet, blooming flowers. God, he didn't remember the last time he'd noticed the scent of a woman.

He consciously focused back on the issue at hand. "I realized that it didn't look like the dogs in the yard had been fed and watered, so I took care of them and then left. Same thing happened yesterday. I was worried that maybe she was sick, so I used my key to come inside. I fed and watered Zeus and the dogs outside and then went back home."

He frowned thoughtfully. "I haven't known your sister for very long, but this felt out of character for her. I was worried, and then tonight when I realized somebody was in the house, I decided to come in and investigate."

He didn't feel it was necessary to tell her that when he'd seen that pink streak in her hair before she'd completely turned around to face him, he'd thought she was one of the teenagers of the town taking advantage of Lauren's absence for an opportunity for a little party or a bit of theft.

"This is definitely out of character for Lauren," she said and finally laid her gun down on the table next to her. "What's your relationship with her? Romantic?"

"Not at all," he replied. "Over the last couple of months Lauren and I have become good friends, but nothing more than that."

"Her truck is in the garage."

It took him a second to adjust to the leap in topic and

her words sent a vague sense of uneasiness through him. "I didn't know that."

She nodded. "I checked out the property. Zeus and I walked it looking for her, but needless to say we didn't find her." She stood abruptly. "Thank you for looking out for things here."

It was an obvious dismissal and Nick stood and grabbed his shotgun as she started out of the kitchen. He followed just behind her and tried not to notice the cute shape of her butt in her tight jeans.

What was wrong with him? He was far too conscious of Lexie Forbes's attractiveness and it made him more than a little bit uncomfortable.

Maybe part of the problem was even though he knew Lauren and Lexie were identical twins, the woman in front of him seemed more vibrant and much prettier than her sister.

"So, what's your next move?" he asked as they reached the front door.

She frowned. "First thing in the morning if she doesn't come home or I don't hear from her, I'll head into town and file a missing persons report at the police station."

"Don't expect much from the local authorities," he replied, remembering a time when he'd filed his own missing person's report and nothing had been done until it was too late.

She looked at him sharply. "Why? Is there a problem?"

"I went to high school with Gary Wendall, the chief

of police. He tends toward big talk and little action." Nick's stomach knotted at thoughts of Wendall, who had been damned little help when Nick had needed him most.

"I'll file the report and then I'm going to ask questions and see if I can find out who might have last seen Lauren and when. I spoke to her Tuesday night so I know she was here and fine then."

She looked up at him and in the depths of her pretty green eyes he saw fear. "She's all I have. I have to find her," she said, her voice husky with emotion.

He had a crazy sudden impulse to pull her into his arms, to assure her that everything was going to be just fine. Instead he opened up the door, flipped on the outside porch light and then stepped out.

She followed him, her gaze automatically scanning the area as if hoping her sister would suddenly appear in the illuminated spill of the high-powered beam of light.

"I'd like it if you'd keep me informed," he said and then frowned. "I should have given you my cell phone number."

"Give it to me now," she replied.

"You don't have any place to write it down," he protested.

"I'll remember it."

Although dubious, he rattled off the number. When he was finished she nodded. "I'll let you know if I find out anything or if she turns up here."

"I'd appreciate it. I guess I'll talk to you soon." He

stepped off the porch, and as she murmured a goodbye he headed for his pickup in the driveway.

When he got into the truck, he gazed at her once again. Lexie Forbes affected him like no other woman had in a very long time.

Despite the circumstances of their meeting he was surprised to realize what he'd felt for her was a momentary flare of desire.

He shook his head and started his truck, focusing his thoughts back on the missing Lauren. There was no question that mutual loneliness had forged their friendship over the last couple of months. She'd been new in town, hadn't known anyone, and he'd been mired in grief for so long he'd become isolated from everyone else.

Lauren had been easy to talk to, pleasant to be around, but he'd told Lexie the truth when he'd said there had been nothing romantic between them.

There would never be romance in Nick's life again. He'd had his one great love with tragic results. His heart would forever remain unavailable to any other woman on the face of the earth.

He headed down the road to the farmhouse that no longer felt like home, but was rather just a place to sleep and eat, a place to exist.

That's all he'd been doing for a long time—existing and marking time. Lauren had definitely helped pass the time, especially the evening hours after dinner and before bedtime.

Still, as he thought of Lauren he was filled with

a sense of dread, that somehow history was repeating itself. He couldn't stop thinking that the last time a woman had disappeared for a couple of days she'd wound up dead in a motel room.

Chapter Two

The night had been endless.

Before going to bed Lexie had found a local phone book and called the hospital and the clinics in the area, but none of them would admit to having Lauren as a patient. Surely if she was in the hospital somebody would have called Lexie by now. Lexie was listed as Lauren's emergency contact.

The only thing that made Lexie feel a little bit better was that she couldn't find Lauren's purse or her cell phone in the house. She could only assume Lauren had those items with her wherever she was.

Still, by the time morning had come Lexie's eyes felt gritty from lack of sleep. She had tried to rest in the guest room, but had finally ended up on the sofa with Zeus on the floor next to her.

Every sound the house had made through the night, every creak and whisper shot her up with the hope that it might be Lauren returning home. At 5:00 a.m. she finally gave up any pretense of sleep and went into the spare bedroom that Lauren used as an office.

She powered up the computer on the desk. Knowing

that Lauren used Zeus20 as a password, she checked the email to see if there was anything that might explain her sister's absence.

Most of the correspondence was business related, emails from potential customers asking about her dogs and her training. Others were from past customers catching Lauren up on news of some of the dogs she'd trained.

She also checked the history to see where Lauren might have gone on the internet, but found nothing that might yield a clue as to what had happened to her.

She drained her coffee cup and then began a search of the desk. A stack of file folders in a plastic holder drew her attention and she pulled them out to see what they contained.

They were contracts signed by the people whose dogs Lauren was training. There was one signed by Nick, who had been bringing his dog for obedience training.

Her head filled with a vision of the man she'd met the night before. Hot body, sensual lips and a hint of compassion in his bedroom eyes—the man could definitely be an unwanted distraction if she allowed it.

She focused back on the folders, surprised to discover that one of them contained a contract for Lauren to provide the Topeka Police Department with two drug-sniffing dogs.

She leaned back in the desk chair as a surge of pride mingled with surprise. She'd known that Lauren had wanted to get into the training of working dogs, especially for law enforcement and handicapped people.

From the signed contract, Lexie assumed that Lauren was truly on the way to making a name for herself, on her way to achieving her dreams.

It was almost seven when she finished in Lauren's office and took a quick shower. She dressed in a pair of jeans and a neon pink blouse decorated with an abundance of sequins and then returned to the kitchen to pour herself another cup of coffee.

As soon as it was late enough she was heading into town. Her first stop was going to be the police station to file a missing persons report, and then she planned on talking to everyone and anyone to pin down the last time her sister had been seen.

The fear that had been inside her hadn't dissipated, but rather thrummed like a sick energy inside her chest. Throughout the long night she'd tried calling Lauren's cell phone over and over again but it had always gone directly to voice mail. Finally by that morning she'd gotten the message that Lauren's voice mail was full.

Zeus walked over to her and laid his big head on her knee, gazing up at her as if asking her why his mommy wasn't there. "I know, baby. I miss her, too."

Zeus barked and raced away from her as a knock fell on the door. Lexie jumped out of her chair and grabbed her gun from her purse. She knew she was probably overreacting, but she had no idea what to expect, was definitely out of her comfort zone.

When she got to the front door she saw Nick standing on the porch. "What are you doing here?" she asked without preamble as she opened the screen door.

"I thought you could use a friendly face when you go into town this morning." He stepped past her and into the foyer, then turned back to look at her expectantly.

She wouldn't have thought it possible but the man was better looking in the light of day than he'd been the night before. Once again he wore a pair of jeans that looked custom-made for his long legs and narrow hips. His gray long-sleeved pullover clung to his broad shoulders and perfectly matched the hue of his eyes.

"That's not necessary," she said and tried to ignore the ridiculous flutter that went off in the pit of her stomach. This man and her reaction to him were the last things she needed right now. All she wanted, all she needed, was her sister.

"I know Sheriff Wendall. It would probably work to your benefit if I'm with you. And, if you want to ask questions of the people in Widow Creek you'll find that they don't take kindly to strangers."

"Why is that?"

He looked at her in surprise. "I don't know. I guess because we're a small town and we've always looked after our own. Lexie, I was born and raised here—people know me. They trust me and that means they'll talk to me. You're a big-city woman with…uh…" His voice trailed off.

"A pink streak in my hair," she jumped in to finish his sentence. "And it was purple before that." She raised her chin as if to challenge him to say anything derogatory.

"And I'm sure it looked as charming as the pink," he replied.

She eyed him dubiously. What was his story? Why the offer to help her? Was he just a nice guy or had his relationship with Lauren been something deeper than a friendship? She wasn't sure she trusted him, but what he'd said about getting answers made sense. People would probably talk to him much quicker than they would to her.

"Don't you have a wife or somebody at home who might not want you wasting your time with me?" she asked.

"No wife, no girlfriend, just livestock," he replied. "And a little miniature schnauzer puppy who is probably chewing on my best pair of boots as we speak." He smiled then and the warmth and attractiveness of it fired a crazy flame deep inside Lexie.

She ignored it. Any woman would have to be dead not to find Nick Walker extremely hot, but Lexie had learned about hot men and cold hearts the hard way. And, besides, she had a sister to find.

"If you want to tag along, then I'd appreciate your help," she finally agreed. "Just let me get my purse and I'll be ready to go."

She went back into the guest room where she'd left her things and grabbed her purse. Before leaving the room she checked to make sure her gun was inside. Right now she believed Nick was probably okay, but in her line of work she didn't take anything for granted.

She'd travel with her gun in her purse while she was here in Widow Creek.

Minutes later they were in her car and heading into the heart of the small town. The first thing Lexie noticed when they reached Main Street was that Widow Creek was a town obviously dying a slow death.

Half of the storefronts along the two-block main drag were boarded up. The ones that were still opened looked worn and faded, as if it was nothing more than sheer hope keeping them alive.

A half a dozen cars were parked in front of the Cowboy Corral, either attesting to good food or the fact that there was no place else to go to eat and spend a little time among friends.

"The police station is up ahead," Nick said, breaking the silence that had filled the car on the drive from Lauren's place. Lexie wasn't good at small talk and Nick seemed at ease with the quiet. "It's that two-story brick building," he said, pointing to it.

Lexie pulled into a parking spot in front of the station, cut her engine and then turned to look at the man in the passenger seat. "Before we go in there, are you sure you don't want to tell me anything else about your relationship with Lauren?"

His dark eyebrows rose in surprise. "I already told you about my relationship with her. We had become good friends."

"And nothing more?"

"Nothing more," he said firmly.

"Then why are you helping me?"

"I don't know what kind of world you live in with your FBI work, Lexie, but in my world when a friend goes missing you do whatever you can to help find her." He opened the car door and got out.

Lexie hurriedly followed and before they got to the door she grabbed him by the arm. "I think it would be best if we don't mention what I do for a living," she said. It had been her experience that people didn't talk freely to an FBI agent, that they would be more likely to talk to a worried sister. Small-town law enforcement was known to be rather hostile to FBI agents. The last thing she wanted was to upset the police chief when she needed his help. "If anybody asks, I do web design for a living."

He nodded. "Okay, but you know it's possible Lauren mentioned to others here in town what you do for a living. I knew."

She considered what he said. "Then we'll just play it by ear, but I don't intend to volunteer any information about myself unless it's absolutely necessary."

As they walked through the door of the police station Lexie's fear for her sister spiked nearly out of control. What could have happened to her? Where could she be?

Filing an official missing persons report suddenly made Lauren's disappearance more real, far more frightening. For the first time since they'd left the house Lexie was grateful that Nick was beside her. Even though she didn't know him well, his presence made her feel not quite so all alone.

"Hey, Carol," he greeted the woman behind the receptionist desk.

"Nick!" The pretty blonde looked up from her computer and offered him an inviting smile that definitely spoke of feminine interest. Her gaze slid over Lexie, the calculating look of a woman checking out her competition. She obviously wasn't concerned by what she saw. She dismissed Lexie with a flick of her false lashes.

Nick returned the smile and gestured toward the closed office door behind her desk. "Is Gary in?"

"Should be on his second donut by now," she replied wryly. "You can go on in."

Lexie followed behind Nick as he approached the closed office door and knocked. A deep voice indicated they could come in.

Chief of Police Gary Wendall sat at the desk, but rose as they entered. He looked to be in his early thirties, with blond military-short hair and a fit physique. "Nick, it's been a while," he said, and in his words Lexie thought she heard a touch of tension. The two men shook hands and then Wendall looked at Lexie.

"Chief Wendall, I'm Lexie Forbes. I'm here about my sister, Lauren Forbes."

"Ah, our very own dog whisperer," Wendall said with a nod. "What about her?"

"She's missing." Sudden emotion filled Lexie's chest and she had to swallow hard against it.

Wendall motioned them into the chairs in front of his desk and then sat down. "What do you mean she's missing?"

"I spoke to her Tuesday night on the phone, but I couldn't get hold of her Wednesday or Thursday," Lexie explained. "Finally yesterday evening I decided to drive out to her place. She's not there and I don't think she's been there since Tuesday. Her dogs were left unattended and that's not like her. Something has happened. Something is terribly wrong."

"Whoa, let's not jump to conclusions," Wendall exclaimed, lines cutting into his tanned forehead. "She's a grown woman. There's no law that says she can't take off for a couple of days without checking in with anyone."

Lexie shook her head. "She wouldn't do that, and even if she did she'd answer my phone calls. We talk to each other every day. This is unusual for her...for us. I want to file a missing persons report. She's been missing more than forty-eight hours. I need you to investigate her disappearance."

Wendall's gaze flickered from Lexie to Nick. "What's your role in all this?"

"I'm Lauren's friend and I'm concerned, and I'm here to support Lexie," Nick replied. His voice held a coolness that definitely chilled the air in the room.

"You aren't stirring things up because of your own history?" Wendall asked with a lift of one of his blond eyebrows.

Lexie looked at Nick and saw the tightening of his jaw as his eyes went flat. "One thing has nothing to do with the other," he replied tersely.

There was obviously some personal history between

the two men, but Lexie didn't care about that right now. All she cared about was finding her sister.

"Will you look into this?" she asked Wendall. "Start an official investigation?"

"I'll see what I can do," Wendall replied. "Are you staying out at Lauren's place?"

Lexie nodded. "I'll be there until she's found." She gave him her cell phone number and then walked toward the door. There was nothing more to be done here. She wanted to get outside and walk the streets, talk to the people in town and see if anyone had seen or spoken to Lauren since Tuesday.

"I'll keep in touch," Chief Wendall said as she and Nick reached the door. "You know your sister always had a bunch of men hanging around her place. Maybe she took off with one of them and didn't want you knowing about her personal affairs," Wendall said.

Lexie stiffened and stared at him. At that moment she decided she didn't like him very much. He made it sound like Lauren was some kind of a whore. "I'm sure you're going to question whatever men were hanging out there to see what they know about my sister's disappearance," she replied.

She was surprised when Nick firmly took hold of her elbow, as if to offer support, as they left the office. What equally surprised her was how she responded to his touch—viscerally, like a not-completely-unpleasant punch in the stomach.

As they left the building he dropped his hand to his side and she drew a breath of relief. She didn't want some crazy attraction to Nick complicating things. The last thing she wanted in her life was a man. She just wanted to find her sister alive and well, and then get back to her so-called life in Kansas City.

"I never saw a bunch of men hanging out at Lauren's," Nick said when they were back in her car. "And I drove by her place at least once a day going to and from town. But she mentioned to me that she was kind of seeing Bo Richards."

"Bo Richards?" Lexie turned in her seat to look at Nick. "Who is he?"

"He's a local rancher, a nice guy. He spends a lot of time in the mornings at the café. Maybe we can talk to him there," Nick replied.

"And Lauren was seeing him romantically?" Lexie frowned. Her sister hadn't mentioned anything to her about a romance in her life and they'd always talked about everything, including their love lives.

"They had just started dating. From what Lauren told me it wasn't real serious yet. I think they'd met for lunch or dinner a couple of times."

Lexie checked her watch and then looked down the street at the café. It was still early. Hopefully they'd find him there. "Then I want to talk to him." She started the car, but before backing out she turned to look at Nick once again. "There's some history between you and Wendall?"

Darkness filled his eyes and his jaw tightened once again. "Yeah, old history."

"Want to tell me about it?" she asked.

"No." The single word snapped out of him with a finality that brooked no further questions and made Lexie wonder what kind of secrets Nick Walker had in his life.

IN THE SHORT DISTANCE between the police station and the Cowboy Corral, painful memories cascaded through Nick's head. His chest tightened with thoughts of the three days that he'd been unable to get in contact with Danielle. His body remembered intimately the alarm it had felt when he'd realized nobody had seen her during that time and the horror of ultimately finding her dead in that motel room.

His stomach clenched and a slight nausea rose up in him as the memories continued to play in his head. He'd known something was wrong—that something was terribly wrong.

It had taken him months to finally accept that she'd committed suicide, but before coming to that acceptance he'd gone around and around with Wendall.

The chief of police had dismissed Nick's concerns and refused to begin any kind of investigation into Danielle's disappearance despite Nick pressing for one. There was part of Nick that had never quite forgiven Gary Wendall for that.

He consciously shoved the memories aside as Lexie parked in front of the café. There was absolutely no reason to believe Lauren's disappearance was in any way connected to Danielle's tragic death, but he couldn't shake the feeling that Lexie was destined for the same kind of heartbreak he'd suffered.

Still suffered.

He willed away all thoughts of Danielle as they got out of the car. Lexie appeared small and achingly vulnerable as she hesitated outside the door to wait for him to catch up with her.

A surge of unexpected protectiveness filled Nick's chest. It was crazy, he scarcely knew Lexie except for what Lauren had told him about her. There was no reason for him to be emotionally vested in the drama going on in her life, and yet for some reason he was definitely involved.

He told himself it had nothing to do with the beauty of her long-lashed green eyes behind those ridiculously large glasses, nothing to do with the fact that she intrigued him more than a little bit. Rather he tried to convince himself his interest in all this had everything to do with finding a woman who had become a good friend.

The minute they stepped into the café, every head in the place turned to look at them. "I guess pink streaks in a person's hair isn't that common here," Lexie muttered beneath her breath as she sidled closer to him.

"Don't worry, the only ones who bite have no teeth," he replied.

She looked up at him and smiled. It was the first real smile he'd seen from her and it nearly stole his breath away. Bright and beautiful, it transformed her features into something more than pretty, something warm and inviting.

"Come on, I'm hankering for some of Mabel's fried potatoes and eggs." He took her beneath her elbow and led her to a booth, surprised to realize she was shaking slightly.

Lauren had told him that her sister didn't do well in crowds. He knew the effort she was putting forth was because of her love and concern for her sister. It only made him more determined to support her through whatever happened next.

She paused before sitting down and looked around at the other diners. "I thought we'd just ask some questions. I didn't plan on actually having a meal."

"Did you eat breakfast this morning?" he asked.

"I never eat breakfast," she replied.

"And you've never had a missing sister before," he said and pointed to the booth. "Besides, you'll get more answers to questions if we finesse them out of people."

She frowned as if she had no idea what he was talking about, but slid into the booth and picked up the menu. She stared at it only a minute and then tossed it aside. "I feel like I'm wasting time here. Breakfast isn't important. Finding Lauren is all that matters." Her voice held a wealth of frustration and impatience.

"You have to eat," he replied, understanding the urgency that was racing through her. "And you have to trust me." He looked up as the waitress appeared at their table. "Hey, Marge, how's it going?" he asked the older woman who had been waitressing at the café since he'd been a little boy.

"Like it's always gone. My feet hurt, my back is killing me and nobody tips worth a damn in this place." She flashed him a grin that set the deep wrinkles in her face dancing.

"Has Bo been in today?" he asked.

"Bo? No, in fact, I haven't seen him for a couple of days." Her gaze slid to Lexie. "Why? Is there a problem?"

"No, no problem," he replied hurriedly. "Marge, this is Lauren Forbes's sister, Lexie."

Marge nodded. "I can see the resemblance."

"When was the last time you saw Lauren?" Lexie asked.

Marge looked back at Nick, her eyes narrowed. "What's going on, Nick?"

Nick could feel Lexie's frustration growing by the second, but he ignored her. "Lexie's in town to visit her sister, but Lauren seems to have gone missing and we're trying to hunt her down. Has she been in lately?"

Marge frowned. "I think she was in Monday for lunch, but I haven't seen her since then. Now, what can I get for the two of you?"

They ordered and once Marge left the table Lexie released a deep sigh. "That was no help. We need to question everyone in here, see who saw Lauren when."

"Just sit tight. Trust me when I tell you before we finish our breakfast you'll have spoken to everyone in this place." He could tell that she didn't believe him but she settled back in the booth, took her glasses off and rubbed at her eyes. "Not much sleep last night?" he asked sympathetically.

Her eyes were the most amazing shade of green with just enough shadow in them to be slightly mysterious. "I don't think I slept much more than an hour through the whole night." She slid the glasses back on. "I just can't wrap my head around this." Her gaze held a hint of vulnerability as she looked at him. "I'm scared."

He could tell what the confession cost her by the way her gaze skittered away from his and from the telltale pulse of a delicate vein in her neck. Before he could respond Jim Caskie ambled by the table to say hello to Nick.

It was just as he'd suspected—as they ate their breakfast almost everyone who was dining in the café found a reason to stop by and say hello. Lexie merely picked at her eggs and nibbled on toast, more interested in what people had to say than in the meal in front of her.

Nick knew the people of Widow Creek were leery of strangers, but he also knew they were a curious bunch. And Lexie, with the pink streak in her hair and her pink sequined blouse definitely sparked plenty of curiosity.

The one thing that didn't happen was answers. Nobody had seen Lauren since Monday, at least nobody who would admit to it. And nobody had seen Bo for the past couple of days. This information eased some of Nick's concern.

Even the most levelheaded women occasionally went crazy over a man. It was possible the two had gone off

together for a romantic tryst and Lauren had just forgotten to make arrangements for her dogs or had wound
up being gone longer than she'd initially planned.

"Do you know where Bo lives?" Lexie asked the
minute they were back in her car.

"Yeah, you want to go by there?" He wasn't surprised
when she nodded her head.

After giving her directions, he tried to think of
something, anything, he could tell her that might ease
some of the tension that rode her slender shoulders and
darkened her eyes.

"So, Lauren told me you're something of a computer
geek," he finally said, wanting to connect with her on a
more personal level. "What exactly is it that you do?"

"I work for the cybercrime unit for the FBI. Mostly
I hunt down cybercriminals, those who are invading
home computers to steal identities, and I try to find the
source behind thousands of scams that people receive
via email."

"Sounds fascinating."

She flashed him a quick glance. "Most people would
find it pretty boring, but I like it. I'm comfortable working with a computer. It's predictable. I type in code and
I know what's going to happen."

"Unlike people, who can be unpredictable," he observed.

"Exactly." She chewed her bottom lip and for just a
minute he wondered what it would be like to taste her
mouth with his. The thought flashed in his head with a
shock. He had no business even thinking such thoughts.

What was wrong with him? He hadn't entertained such a thought about a woman in years.

She was here to find her sister and nothing more. In any case, he was mentally and emotionally unavailable to any woman when it came to his heart.

Still, he grudgingly admitted that perhaps his momentary fantasy about the taste of her mouth meant that he wasn't quite as dead as he'd believed himself to be.

They pulled up in front of Bo's place and she cut the engine as she stared at the neat two-story house before them. The front door was closed and there were no vehicles around. "Looks like nobody is home," he said.

"You can wait here. I'll go find out." She got out of the car and walked toward the front door.

Nick remained in the car, his gaze following the slight sway of her hips. Okay, he could admit to himself that he was sexually attracted to her. There was no real explanation for the immediate physical chemistry he felt toward her.

Of course, it had been almost two years since he'd been with a woman. Maybe this was just his body's way of reminding him that he was a healthy thirty-three-year-old man who had been alone for too long. In any case, it wasn't something he intended to act upon, just a curious surprise that reminded him that he was very much alive.

He watched as Lexie knocked on the front door several times, then moved to peek through the living room windows and finally returned to the car.

"He's not here. Maybe she did go off with him for a couple of days," she said.

"Women have been known to momentarily lose their minds for love," he replied.

"Not me," she replied darkly. "Not ever."

She started the car and pulled out of the driveway. "I'm going back into town to ask more questions, but I'll be glad to drop you off at your place. I'm sure you have better things to do than spend the day with me."

"Actually, I don't." There was nothing for him at home except the endless silence and loneliness that had gnawed at his heart for the past year. "If two of us are asking questions then we can get it done in half the time."

She eyed him for a long moment and then shrugged. "Suit yourself."

The remainder of the ride back into town was silent. Nick couldn't begin to guess what she was thinking. He didn't know her well enough, but he was surprised to realize that he wished he did.

They stayed in town throughout the afternoon, drifting into stores, stopping people on the streets and asking about Lauren. By five o'clock it was clear that Lauren hadn't been seen by anyone since Tuesday.

Nick still held out hope that she and Bo had taken off on some sort of romantic connection, but he could see with each minute that passed that Lexie was growing more distraught.

She nibbled on her lower lip and looked tense enough to shatter if anyone would reach out and touch her. He finally called a halt. "It's time to go home, Lexie," he said. "You've done all you can do for today and you're only getting the same answers over and over again."

For a moment he thought she was going to protest, but then her shoulders fell and she nodded wearily. "You're right. It's been a long day and we aren't getting anywhere."

Once again she was quiet on the ride back to Lauren's and Nick wished he had some encouraging words to give her. But there was no question that Lauren's disappearance was troubling. As the day had worn on his hope that she'd gone off with Bo had faded. If that was the case, then why hadn't she returned Lexie's phone calls? Why didn't she answer her cell phone? Surely she'd know that Lexie would be worried sick.

They had gotten one piece of information from one of Bo's neighbors who told them that Bo had mentioned visiting some family in Tulsa, Oklahoma. If Bo was with family in Oklahoma, then where was Lauren? The whole thing was growing more and more troubling with each minute that passed.

"Thanks for your help today," Lexie said as she pulled up next to his truck in Lauren's driveway. She stared at the house as if dreading going inside.

"Look, we haven't eaten since breakfast. Why don't I take you out to dinner?"

She turned to look at him. "Why would you want to do that?"

He shrugged. "Because I need to eat. You need to

eat and we might as well eat together. Why don't I pick you up in an hour?"

She turned and looked at the house again, a frown pulling together her delicately arched eyebrows. "I have a bad feeling about this, Nick. I don't think she's ever coming home."

He reached across the seat and took her hand in his. "You can't lose hope already," he said softly. "Maybe she took off with Bo and her cell phone went dead. That would explain her not answering your calls." Her hand felt small in his grasp.

She stared at him as if desperate to believe his words. "Maybe you're right," she finally conceded. She pulled her hand from his. "I guess I'll see you in an hour."

They both got out of her car and Nick stood by his truck and watched her walk to the house. There was no question that something about Lexie touched him in a place where nobody had touched him in a very long time.

There was an awkwardness about her that he found oddly charming. The pink streak in her hair spoke of a woman seeking attention and yet he'd never seen a woman who appeared more uncomfortable with any attention she garnered.

As he got into his truck he wondered what in the hell he was doing. He'd spent the day with her and now had invited her to dinner, as if he couldn't get enough of her company.

And yet he knew nothing could come of his attraction to her. She'd given him no indication that she felt the same kind of attraction to him that he did for her, and even if she did he wouldn't follow through on it.

He'd had the one great love of his life and he'd blown it and the consequences had been devastating. He was responsible for his wife's suicide, and he'd never allow himself to get close to a woman again.

Chapter Three

She shouldn't have agreed to dinner, Lexie thought as she entered the house. She shouldn't have agreed to dinner with *him*. Nick Walker definitely made her slightly nervous, although she'd been grateful for his presence during the long day.

Still, she should have thanked him for his time and let it go at that. She didn't need the distraction of spending time with a man who made her just a little bit breathless when he gazed at her, a man who made her feel a strange mix of both anxiety and anticipation.

And yet she didn't consider calling him to tell him to forget dinner. She had to eat and she'd rather do it someplace else, anyplace else instead of in the horrible quiet of Lauren's kitchen.

Before she did anything else she checked the answering machine in Lauren's office to see if any calls had come in throughout the day. There was only one from somebody who had apparently stopped by for their appointment with Lauren while Lexie and Nick had been out. The woman, who said her name was Anna, only said that Precious had missed seeing Lauren and asked that Lauren call to reschedule the training session.

Lexie vaguely remembered that when she'd looked through the folder of contracts there had been one signed by an Anna. She made a mental note to contact the woman the next day and let her know that, at least at the moment, Lauren wasn't available for taking appointments.

Zeus followed Lexie to the bathroom where she quickly took off her clothes and stepped into the shower. As she stood beneath the warm spray, her thoughts whirled over what they'd learned that day, which had been darned little.

She still hoped they would discover that Lauren had gone off someplace with Bo Richards and that she'd return home any minute, feeling guilty and sheepish at causing so much unwarranted worry. Maybe she'd made arrangements for somebody to take care of the dogs in her absence and whomever she'd hired had just blown off the job.

She got out of the shower and changed into a clean pair of jeans and a Kelly-green lightweight sweater. Zeus sat at her feet and watched as she applied a light coating of both mascara and lipstick. As she finished with her hair and turned away from the mirror he whined, as if protesting the fact that she was leaving him again.

She checked her watch and realized she had another twenty minutes before Nick would be back to get her. "Come on, baby, let's see if I can find you a treat," she said to the big dog, who followed close at her heels as she went into the kitchen.

She rummaged in the cabinets until she found a bag of pepperoni dog treats. Zeus woofed his approval and she tossed it to him, laughing as he caught it midair.

He ate it and then headed for the doggy door cut into the kitchen wall that led to the fenced in backyard. She moved to the window and watched as the dog romped around in the grass next to the other fenced area and then lifted his leg against a bush.

As much as she wanted to believe that her sister had taken off someplace, it just didn't feel right. Zeus was her baby and Lexie couldn't imagine Lauren just taking off for days and leaving him behind. She would have at least made arrangements for him to be fed and watered by somebody she trusted to do the job.

The ring of the doorbell pulled her from her thoughts. Nervous energy danced in her stomach as she hurried out of the kitchen to the front door.

Nick had showered and changed as well. He wore jeans and a long-sleeved gray dress shirt and, as if his physical attractiveness wasn't enough, he smelled like clean, crisp cologne mixed with the faint residual scent of shaving cream.

"Ready?" he asked.

She nodded. "Just let me grab my purse."

Her heart hammered with inexplicable quickness as she got her purse from the kitchen counter and then rejoined him at the front door. "Ready," she said, knowing that Zeus would return to the house through the doggy door.

The evening was cool as they walked to his car. A slight breeze stirred the autumn leaves on the trees, forcing some of them to drift down to the ground.

Although in her heart for some reason she trusted Nick, in her head she wasn't sure who she could trust. She was comforted by the fact that her purse held her gun and she wouldn't be afraid to use it if things somehow went bad.

"There aren't many eating choices in Widow Creek so I thought we'd drive the twenty minutes to Casey's Corner. It's a slightly bigger town and has a great Italian place," he said as they pulled out of the driveway.

"Sounds fine," she agreed. She wasn't really hungry, hadn't had an appetite since she'd discovered that Lauren was missing, but she knew she had to eat to keep up her strength.

For a few minutes they rode in silence. Lexie stared out the window at the encroaching evening shadows and anxiety pressed tight against her chest. She couldn't believe another night was about to fall without her knowing if Lauren was okay.

"I just can't imagine what's happened to her," she said as much to herself as to him. "I keep thinking maybe she's been hit over the head and is lying someplace needing me to find her."

He gave her a curious glance. "Why would you think that?"

She hesitated, knowing he would probably think she

was crazy for what she was about to say. "Friday, when I got into my car after work to go home, I was struck with a blinding head pain." She raised a hand to the back of her head, remembering that violent, momentary slice of pain. "It was there only a moment and then gone and I immediately wondered if maybe Lauren had gotten hurt."

She dropped her hand back to her lap as a laugh of embarrassment escaped her. "It's kind of a twin thing. One time Lauren broke her arm and I knew it before she told me because I felt her pain in my arm. Another time I broke my little toe and she called me to see what I'd done because her foot hurt." She laughed again without any real humor. "I know it sounds crazy."

"Not really, I saw a documentary one night about twins and the special bond they share. Must have been interesting growing up. Did you two pretend to be each other? Try to fool people?"

Lexie cast her gaze back out the window, her thoughts taking her backward in time. "No, never. From the very beginning, even though we were identical twins, we had completely different personalities. Lauren is an extro-vert and I've always been painfully shy. I could have never made anyone believe that I was her."

She turned to look at him, trying not to notice how handsome he looked with the last gasp of the sun light-ing his features. "When we started high school there was Lauren and then there was the other twin. Nobody could remember my name, nobody really knew who I was. That's when I decided to go Goth."

He gave her an amused smile. "So you dressed in black, wore heavy makeup and spouted tragic poetry."

She returned his smile. "Something like that."

"And did that help the other kids get to know you better?"

"Not really. I went from being the 'other' twin to being the weird twin." It all seemed so silly now, but at the time high school had been the most painful experience Lexie thought she'd ever live through. "It wasn't until I was in college that I realized it was okay to embrace my quirkiness, to be a little different than everyone else."

"We're all quirky in one way or another. Some of us just show it more than others."

"You don't look quirky to me," she observed.

He grinned. "Ah, but looks can be deceiving. I sleep in my socks."

"That's not quirky, that's nerdy," she replied and then gasped at her own words.

He laughed. "That's what I like about you, Lexie. I have a feeling you always speak what's on your mind. And you're right, it is nerdy, but I always have nice warm feet."

She averted her gaze back out the window and tried to cast out the vision of her in his bed, his warm feet against hers, slowly warming her body from her toes upward.

By that time they had reached the town of Casey's Corner. It appeared to be a big sister of Widow Creek.

The business area stretched over three short blocks and there were only a couple of empty storefronts.

He pulled up in front of Mama's Italian Garden and as he parked she realized that the conversation they'd shared on the drive had momentarily taken her mind off Lauren. She suspected that's what he'd intended and a warm gratefulness swelled in her chest.

It took only minutes for them to be seated at a table for two in the restaurant. It was a typical Italian setting, with red-and-white checkered tablecloths, a little candle flickering in the center of the table and a very limited wine list displayed between the salt and pepper shakers.

As Lexie picked up a menu her stomach rumbled with sudden hunger. Maybe it was the aroma of rich tomato sauce and fresh herbs that wafted in the air, or perhaps it was the conversation they'd shared that had relaxed her a bit on the drive to the restaurant.

"I eat here fairly often and can tell you that pretty much anything on the menu is good," Nick said.

She was acutely conscious of his nearness at the small, intimate table. His eyes glowed almost silver in the candlelight and she found herself wondering what his lips might taste like.

She snapped her focus down to the menu, wondering if the stress of everything was making her lose her mind. She'd given up on men almost six months ago when she'd discovered that the man she'd believed was "the one" turned out to be "the rat."

Michael Andrews had been a smooth-talking, hot-looking guy who had swept Lexie off her feet and away from her computer. They'd met through a mutual friend and they'd dated for six months. Lexie had thought they were moving toward an engagement, but instead she'd found out that Michael had a woman on the side, a cute, bubbly blonde who was all the things that Lexie wasn't, that Lexie would never be.

"Face it, Lexie," he had said. "You're a little bit weird. It was fun for a while but I wouldn't want a steady diet of it."

She'd mentally dug a hole and buried her hopes for happily-ever-after in it and had returned to a social life that involved cyberfriends who didn't have the capacity to hurt her.

Nick reminded her just a little bit of Michael. Maybe because he was good-looking and seemed to know exactly what she wanted to hear when she wanted to hear it.

The waitress appeared at their table and Nick ordered lasagna while Lexie opted for the manicotti. "Lauren told me the two of you were raised by your father," he said once the waitress had departed.

She nodded. "Our mom died in a car accident when we were four. Dad was devastated, but he rose to the challenge of raising us." A pang of grief touched her heart as she thought of her dad. He'd been her rock and she missed him desperately.

"He didn't remarry?" Nick asked.

"No." She picked up her water glass and took a drink, then continued, "He told us that mom was his one great love and he had no desire to be with anyone else."

"Ah, the one arrow theory."

She looked at him curiously. "One arrow theory?"

"Some people believe that Cupid has one true arrow for everyone. If you're lucky when that arrow hits you, you're with your soul mate and you're together and happy for the rest of your life."

"That's a nice theory, but it doesn't account for Cupid's misfires," she said dryly.

His eyes sparkled with a light that threatened to draw her into their depths. "But if you believe in the one arrow theory, Cupid doesn't misfire, and people often misinterpret and think it's a real arrow that has struck their heart. I assume from your comment that you haven't been struck by Cupid's magic arrow yet."

Lexie thought about her relationship with Michael. Had she truly been in love with him? She'd certainly thought so at the time, but since their parting of ways, she had become equally certain that Michael hadn't been her soul mate. In the very depths of her heart, she wasn't sure there was a soul mate for her on the face of the earth.

"No," she finally replied. "I don't think Cupid's arrow has connected with me."

The conversation was interrupted by the arrival of the waitress with their orders. The food looked delicious and tasted just as good. "So, you said you grew up in Widow Creek. Have you always ranched?" she asked after enjoying several bites.

"Always," he replied. "The house where I live was my parents'. They decided to enjoy early retirement in

Florida and so I bought the place from them. I thought it would be nice for my kids to be raised in the same house where I'd had such happiness."

"But you don't have a wife so I'm assuming there are no children yet."

His eyes darkened, the twinkling silver lights in the center dousing like candle flames that had been blown out. "I had a wife and almost had a child but then everything exploded apart."

Lexie stared at him as grief stole over his handsome features. She set down her fork, the food in front of her temporarily forgotten. "What happened?"

For a moment he stared down at his plate as if lost in thought, and when he looked up at her again some of the grief had passed and weariness lined his face. "I was twenty-five when I married my high school sweetheart and we moved to my parents' ranch to start our lives together. Danielle and I were a perfect couple. I worked the ranch and she worked in the mayor's office and things were terrific. After a couple of years of marriage we decided it was time to start a family. It took almost three years for Danielle to get pregnant. We were so excited when it finally happened."

He paused and took a sip of his water. Lexie felt a tightness in her chest. She knew something bad was coming and even though she'd only known him for a day her heart already ached for him.

As he placed his glass back on the table she noticed his fingers trembled slightly. "When Danielle was eight months pregnant she went in for her usual checkup and the doctor couldn't hear the baby's heartbeat. The doctor decided she needed to deliver immediately so Danielle was hospitalized and labor was induced. Ten hours later she delivered a beautiful stillborn baby girl."

Lexie released a small gasp. "I'm so sorry." She fought the impulse to reach across the table and take his hand in hers. "Did they know what caused it?"

He shook his head. "One of those tragic medical mysteries." He straightened his shoulders. "Anyway, I took Danielle and we went home to get on with our lives." He eyed Lexie intently, beseechingly. "She was so depressed, and I tried to do everything in my power to be supportive, but it seemed like no matter what I did or said it was wrong. After six months she told me she needed some space and she moved into an apartment in town."

"So, you not only lost your child, but your wife as well," Lexie said, working to speak around the lump in her throat.

He leaned back in the chair and released a deep sigh. "Actually, four months after the separation we began to see each other again."

For a moment his features lifted and a small smile curved his lips. "It was just like old times and we started talking about a reconciliation. She seemed to have moved past her grief and was ready to start living again." The smile dropped from his lips. "And then she disappeared."

"Disappeared?" Lexie's heart slammed into her ribs.

Was he implying that there was some sort of connection between his ex-wife and her sister?

"She was gone for three days and during that time I went to Gary Wendall to file a missing persons report." His eyes darkened with a steely light. "And he basically told me the same thing he told you, that it wasn't a crime for a grown woman to take off. He also told me that everyone knew Danielle and I had a troubled history and she'd left me and maybe she just didn't want to be found by me. But I knew something was terribly wrong. Three days later her body was found in a motel room."

Once again a small gasp escaped Lexie, but before she could say anything he continued. "She had a fatal gunshot wound to her head and it was officially ruled a suicide."

Lexie searched his face. "But you didn't believe the official ruling."

His shoulders slumped slightly. "Initially no. I didn't believe that Danielle would take her own life. She didn't believe in suicide. She thought it was a mortal sin. Before she disappeared she'd had the old spark of life back in her eyes, had made me believe that we still had a chance together. I told Gary my concerns, insisted he launch a full-blown investigation into her death, but he dismissed me. Everyone knew how depressed she had been and there was absolutely no evidence to prove it was anything but a suicide. Eventually I realized Gary was probably right, that I just hadn't seen how depressed Danielle still was and she'd finally decided to end it."

Lexie had no words. The depth of his tragedy left her

utterly speechless. He leaned forward and gave a small laugh. "Terrible dinner conversation. I don't know why I decided to share that with you."

"When did all this happen?" She finally found her voice.

"Danielle died a little over a year ago." He picked up his fork once again and gestured toward her plate. "I hope I didn't completely kill your appetite."

"Maybe just a little," she admitted. She picked up her own fork, her gaze lingering on his face, on the deep gray of his eyes. "Was Danielle your one true Cupid's arrow?"

"Yeah, she was. What we had doesn't come twice in a lifetime. As far as love is concerned, I'm done. But, I found your sister to be a good friend. We spent a lot of evenings together sitting on her front porch and just talking about life."

Despite her worry about Lauren and the sad conversation they'd just shared, Lexie couldn't help the smile that curved her lips. "There's nothing Lauren likes better than sitting around and talking about life. She analyzes and speculates and ruminates about everything."

"And you don't?"

She shrugged. "Life is what it is and talking about it rarely changes things."

"You are very different from your sister."

She smiled. "I think I've subconsciously worked hard to be different from her. That's the way I've found my own identity apart from the twin thing." Her smile faltered and she looked down at her plate. The idea of something happening to Lauren scared her not only because she loved her sister more than anyone else on the planet, but also because she was afraid that if Lauren was gone, somehow she would disappear as well.

Lauren was the mirror Lexie used to see her own reflection. If that mirror disappeared then Lexie wasn't sure who she would be anymore.

For the rest of the meal light conversation prevailed. Nick entertained her with stories of his childhood, making her laugh as he related wrestling with calves and saddle breaking a particularly stubborn horse.

He had a wonderful sense of humor and she found it sad that he'd decided he'd had his one great love and wouldn't be looking for another. She had a feeling he would have been a wonderful husband and a terrific father.

"Widow Creek was a great place to grow up," he said as they lingered over dessert. "It was a place where people didn't lock their doors and there was no fear. If you were a kid and did something wrong, half a dozen people would threaten to tell your folks and you knew they would because everyone knew everyone else."

"Sounds like a nice way to grow up."

"It was, but unfortunately Widow Creek has changed with the downswing of the economy. People have moved away to find work, kids no longer return to the town after college but rather choose to make their homes someplace else." He shrugged. "Guess it's happening all over. We're losing our small towns."

By the time they had finished their dessert and were on their way home, her thoughts returned to her sister. "I just can't imagine where Lauren could be," she said thoughtfully.

"Maybe you should bring in some of your FBI friends," he suggested.

"I wish I could. Unfortunately this isn't an FBI matter. It's a matter for the local law enforcement agency." She frowned. "She isn't the type to make enemies, I can't imagine anyone wanting to hurt her."

"I can't either," he agreed. "She didn't know a whole lot of people but she seemed well liked by everyone she did know." He glanced over and to her surprise reached out and lightly touched the back of her hand. "Maybe we'll have the answer when Bo gets back in town."

He pulled his hand back but not before the touch shot a tiny spark and then a wave of heat through her. She tried to ignore her response and breathed a sigh of relief when he pulled up outside Lauren's house.

The house was dark and unwelcoming. She'd forgotten to turn on any lights before she left. A fierce disappointment roared through her as she realized the dark house also implied that Lauren hadn't come home while they'd been out at the restaurant.

"You want me to come in with you?" he asked, as if sensing her uneasiness.

She drew a deep breath. She was uneasy entering the dark house alone, but she was equally uneasy in spending another minute with him. She was far too conscious of him as a man, acutely aware of some crazy attraction she felt toward him.

"No, I'm fine." She opened the car door. "Thanks again for all your time and help today. And thanks for the wonderful meal." She started to get out of the car but paused when he called her name.

"Whatever you need, Lexie. I just want you to know that I'm here to help in whatever way I can."

"I appreciate it, Nick." With a final goodbye she left the car and walked up to the silent, dark house. She fumbled in her purse for the keys, unlocked the front door and then turned on the porch light and waved to Nick.

He finally pulled out of the driveway as Zeus greeted her at the door. "Hi, baby," she said as she scratched the dog behind his ears. He followed her through the house as she turned on lights, her concern for her sister renewing itself with each flip of a switch.

Tomorrow was Sunday, the day she should return to Kansas City to be ready to go back to work on Monday. But there was no way she was leaving here without answers.

She made a call to her supervisor, letting him know that beginning Monday she would be taking some vacation days. Throughout her career with the FBI she'd rarely taken days off for illness or anything else, so her supervisor assured her it wasn't a problem.

Even though it wasn't quite nine o'clock, Lexie went into the guest bedroom and changed into her nightgown. She decided she didn't want to sleep in the bedroom.

She was mentally and physically exhausted and hated that she felt so helpless.

She turned off all the lights in the house except the lamp on the end table next to the sofa and then turned on the television. Zeus circled the floor beside the sofa and then finally flopped down with an audible sigh.

She was way too wound up to go directly to sleep. Worries about Lauren battled with thoughts about Nick, thoughts like what it would feel like to stand in the warmth of his arms, how his mouth would feel pressed hotly, tightly against her own.

Foolish thoughts, she told herself. The last thing she needed in her life was any kind of a hookup with a man who had already told her he'd had his one Cupid arrow and was finished with love. Besides, all she really needed from Nick was his help in finding Lauren.

The dogs woke her, their raucous barking pulling her from a sleep she hadn't realized had claimed her. She shot straight up and grabbed her purse from the coffee table. Her fingers closed around the gun as she rose from the sofa, nerves jangling as the dogs outside in the pen continued to go crazy.

A glance at the clock on the bookcase let her know it was almost two. Zeus was no longer on the floor next to her and as she got up off the sofa her heart banged a frantic rhythm of inexplicable fear.

Instead of going to the front of the house to look out, she went into Lauren's bedroom, knowing that from her sister's window she could see the fenced dog area that ran from the side of the house to the backyard.

In the moonlight she could see that the dogs were at the back of the property, growling and jumping wildly at the fence. She quickly left the bedroom and went to the back door in the kitchen where Zeus stood in front of the door, his hackles raised as deep rumbles issued from his throat.

A cold sweat chilled her; her fingers were damp on the gun. What was out there? Who was out there? Her heart thundered loudly in her ears.

Was it nothing more than a raccoon or a squirrel that had set off the dogs, or was it a person—somebody who might have had something to do with Lauren's disappearance?

She froze as she thought she saw a shadow move from tree to tree in the wooded area beyond the fence. Her heart seemed to stop beating. It wasn't a four-legged creature she'd thought she'd seen. It had been a creature of the two-legged variety. It had been a person.

The dogs stopped barking.

Lexie found the abrupt silence as chilling as the noise. She watched as the dogs drifted away from the fence, as if no longer interested in whatever or whoever had been there.

Zeus released a low growl and then looked up at Lexie with a wag of his tail. He nosed her hand, as if seeking reassurance. "Good boy," she murmured and absently patted his head, her gaze still locked on the woods. The behavior of the dogs indicated to her that whoever had been out there was now gone, but that didn't stop the frantic beat of her heart or the fear that raged through her.

Who had been out there at this time of night? Did the person know what happened to Lauren? She checked to make sure the back door was locked then left the kitchen with Zeus at her side.

Her heart still banged against her ribs as she went through the house, checking doors and windows to make sure everything was locked up tight. Had she only imagined the large shadow moving silently in the night?

Lexie had never considered herself the kind of woman to indulge in flights of fancy or wild imaginings. The real question was: If somebody had been out there, what did they want?

As she sat back on the sofa, she fought a chill that invaded through to her very bones. As if to punctuate her dark thoughts, Zeus released a mournful whine.

Chapter Four

It had taken Nick a long time to go to sleep the night before. He'd been reluctant to call an end to his time with Lexie. She made him feel more alive than he had in a very long time.

He liked the directness of her gaze, the fact that she spoke what was on her mind and seemed not to possess an internal censor. Hell, if he were perfectly honest with himself he'd even admit that he liked the pink streak in her light brown hair.

He sensed a depth of loneliness inside her that called to something deep inside him, but by the time he'd made it home from her house, he was also feeling something else—the heavy weight of guilt.

He now rolled over in his bed and stared at the framed photo on the nightstand next to him. Early morning sunshine poured through the window, making it easy for him to see the picture of the wife he'd lost. Danielle's soft brown eyes seemed to be staring right at him, holding the faintest hint of accusation.

When he'd gotten ready for bed the night before with a desire for Lexie still simmering inside him, he'd gotten the photo of his wife out of the drawer and had placed it there to remind himself that he'd already had his one great love, that somehow, someway he'd managed to screw that up so badly his wife had taken her own life rather than face the rest of her days with him.

She'd killed herself because he'd been unable to give her what she needed, because he hadn't been man enough to take care of her in the way she'd wanted. Somehow, someway, he'd done it all wrong.

He got out of bed before the maudlin thoughts could fully take hold. The sun was up and it was time for him to get started with the morning chores.

The minute his feet hit the floor, Taz, his schnauzer pup, jumped on his toes like a furry ninja who had hidden beneath the bed for the sneak attack.

"Good morning to you, too," he said as he leaned down and scratched Taz behind his ears. The dog barked, his round brown eyes holding more than a hint of mischief.

It took Nick only minutes to pull on a pair of old jeans and a long-sleeved shirt. After a quick cup of coffee he put the leash on Taz and headed outside.

He'd gotten the dog almost four months ago when the silence of the house had been too much to bear. Taz certainly filled the house with energy and had been a loving and often humorous companion. But the little pooch was also incredibly stubborn and had never heard a command he really wanted to obey, which was why Nick had been taking the little guy to Lauren for some basic obedience training.

"I'll be waiting," she replied without hesitation.

Nick tried to tamp down the anticipation that filled him as he grabbed his car keys and then left the house. He told himself that it was simply the possibility of getting some answers from Bo that filled him with anticipation, but he knew in the very center of his heart that it was also because he was going to spend some more time with the woman who unsettled him in a pleasant way.

She was standing on the porch when he pulled up and as he watched she hurried to his truck. She was dressed in a pair of jeans that hugged her slender legs and a bright yellow long-sleeved blouse that made her look fresh and vibrant.

However, as she slid into the passenger seat and he got a look at her eyes, she looked less fresh and more tired. "Bad night, huh?" he asked as he pulled away from Lauren's place.

"The worst yet." She fastened her seat belt and leaned back. "At two this morning somebody was skulking around outside the fence in the backyard."

Nick nearly braked the truck in the middle of the road as he snapped his gaze to her. "Did you see who it was?"

She shook her head. "It was too dark. The dogs barking woke me and all I could see was a shadow moving from tree to tree."

Nick frowned. "It was a human shadow?"

"Definitely."

"Who would be outside at that time of night?"

"That's what I'd like to know. After that it was really hard for me to go back to sleep again. I stayed on the sofa with my gun in my hand, expecting something bad to happen, but nothing did. And now what worries me more than anything is, if Bo Richards is back in town then where is Lauren?"

"Maybe he dropped her off someplace," he offered, although he knew his words were totally lame.

"Yeah, maybe," she said without enthusiasm. "Or maybe Bo and Lauren had some sort of a fight and he killed her and dumped her body on the way to wherever he was going."

Once again Nick fought his impulse to brake at the shock of her words. He found it impossible to even imagine that Bo Richards was capable of murdering a woman, yet he had to remind himself that Lexie didn't know Bo.

"I've got to tell you, I can't imagine Bo being some kind of a killer. He's always seemed to be a nice, even-tempered man who everybody likes," he said. "He's lived here for years and never had any trouble with anyone."

"Yeah, but on the surface Ted Bundy was a nice, pleasant man, too," she replied darkly.

He felt her tension as he pulled up in front of the café. "That's Bo's truck," he said and pointed to the red vehicle two parking spaces from theirs.

As they got out she hurried to the door, as if unable to wait another second to speak to the man she hoped would have some answers about her sister. Nick hurried after her, his heart beating with the rhythm of her anxiety.

Bo sat alone at a booth near the back, a newspaper spread out on the table next to his plate. Nick motioned to Lexie to indicate him and together they wove through the tables to the booth where he sat.

As they reached him, he looked up and smiled. "Hey, Nick." He eyes widened as he gazed at Lexie. "And you have got to be Lauren's sister. Please, sit." He gestured to the seat across from him.

"No, thanks. We just want to ask you a couple of questions," Nick replied.

"Where's my sister?" Lexie blurted. "Where's Lauren?"

Bo lowered the fork he held in his hand and frowned at her. "What do you mean? I would guess she's at home. I just got back into town a little while ago and haven't had a chance to talk to her yet."

"She's been missing since you left town," Nick said.

Bo stared at Nick and then at Lexie. "What do you mean, missing?"

Bo was either a stellar actor or he was as genuinely confused as he looked, Nick thought. "Nobody has seen or heard from Lauren since Tuesday. She left the dogs uncared for and nobody has been able to get in touch with her. We thought maybe she was with you."

"With me? No. I spoke to her Tuesday night before I left town, but I went to visit my parents in Tulsa and my relationship with Lauren hadn't progressed to the point where I felt comfortable taking her with me." He looked at Lexie once again. "We'd just started seeing each other. We haven't had time to get really serious, although I certainly find her company pleasant and would like to keep seeing her."

"Maybe she wanted you to take her with you and you had a fight," Lexie said. She nearly vibrated with energy and Nick realized how desperately she'd hoped Bo would have all the answers.

"Lauren didn't mention wanting to go with me and we had no fight," Bo protested. "You really think I had something to do with Lauren missing? That's crazy."

"When exactly did you leave town, Mr. Richards?" Lexie asked. Her voice trembled slightly and Nick had the feeling she was on the verge of snapping, like a rubber band pulled far too tight.

"My plan was to leave early Wednesday morning, but I was ready to go by around eight Tuesday night and so I went ahead and took off. Have you talked to Gary Wendall about all this?" Bo asked.

"We filed a missing persons report." Nick was aware that they'd garnered the interest of several other people in the café.

He took Lexie by the elbow, knowing that they'd learn nothing more here, but she pulled her arm away from his and stepped closer to the booth.

"Is there anyone who can substantiate your claim that you left here on Tuesday and what time you arrived in Tulsa?" she asked.

"My parents can tell you what time I got there Tuesday night." Bo dug into his pocket and pulled out his wallet. "I even have a gas receipt that will show you that I was on the road to Tulsa Tuesday night." He pulled out a receipt and held it out to Lexie.

Nick noticed that her fingers trembled as she took it from him and stared at it. "Look," Bo continued, "I don't know what to tell you about your sister, but whatever has happened to her, I had absolutely nothing to do with it."

Lexie stared at Bo for several long, agonizing seconds, then handed him back his receipt and looked up at Nick. Her eyes behind the dark-rimmed glasses were large and luminous with barely suppressed emotion. "Let's go," she said. She didn't wait for Nick, but hurried toward the door.

"Nick, I swear I have no idea what's going on with Lauren," Bo exclaimed. "Everything was fine with her when I spoke to her on the phone Tuesday evening before I left town. I'd never do anything to hurt her. I like her!"

Nick nodded and glanced toward the door where Lexie had disappeared from his sight. "Thanks, Bo."

"Let me know what you find out. Now I'm worried," Bo said.

"Will do," Nick replied and then left the booth, eager to catch up with Lexie.

As he stepped outside, he didn't see her either waiting for him outside the door or standing by his truck. He walked toward the truck and then spied her in the doorway of the vacant storefront next to the café.

She looked small and broken, leaning her back

against the window with her shoulders hunched slightly forward. She'd taken off her glasses and held them in one trembling hand. As he approached her, his heart squeezed tight in his chest.

"I didn't realize how much I'd hoped that she was with Bo until now." The tightness in her voice let him know that she was precariously close to losing it. "I believe him. I don't think he had anything to do with Lauren's disappearance." A sob escaped her lips. "Where's my sister, Nick? What's happened to Lauren?"

He could stand it no longer. He closed the short distance between them and took her into his arms. She stood stiff and unyielding for a long moment and then melted against him as she began to weep in earnest.

Although his intent was to simply comfort her, he was acutely aware of the press of her breasts against his chest and of the clean, sweet scent of her that filled his head.

She cried for several minutes. When she finally stopped she didn't move from his arms, but rather remained in his embrace.

She slowly raised her head and looked up at him and her trembling lips seemed to beg him to cover them with his own.

Before he could think, before he could even question his own intent, he lowered his mouth to hers. Hot and sweet, her mouth opened beneath his as he tightened his arms around her.

A greediness filled Nick as his tongue danced with hers. He wanted more of her than a simple kiss. He wanted to feel the weight of her breasts in his palms, her naked legs wrapped with his.

These thoughts stunned him. He wasn't sure who backed away, him or her, but suddenly they stepped back from each other and her gaze held his. In the depth of her bright green eyes he saw a myriad of emotions—shock and embarrassment, but also more than a small flicker of desire.

"I'm sorry," he said, breaking the awkward silence that hung heavily in the air.

"Please, don't apologize. I wanted you to kiss me." She broke the eye contact and slid her glasses back in place. "And now I'd like you to take me back to Lauren's."

Whatever had flared inside her to want him to kiss her was obviously gone as she headed toward his truck. Nick followed behind her, trying to figure out what had just happened between them.

He frowned and forced any thoughts of the kiss out of his head. Instead his thoughts turned to Lauren. He couldn't help but feel that something bad had happened to her.

He had the terrible feeling that heartache and grief were in Lexie's near future and that she was going to need somebody here to lean on. He just had to figure out if he wanted to be her strength or if it was better for the both of them if he completely distanced himself from her.

THE KISS HAD SHAKEN HER almost as much as talking to Bo. By the time Nick had dropped her off at Lauren's place, Lexie was a bundle of screaming nerves.

If she didn't get an answer about Lauren soon she was going to explode. And if she'd spent another minute in Nick's company she felt as if she might blow up as well.

She sank down on the sofa with Zeus at her feet and thought about the man who had just dropped her off. She felt a wild chemistry with him, one that she'd never felt with Michael. It scared her more than just a little bit. She didn't want to feel that way about any man. Nick Walker had heartbreaker written all over him and she'd do well to remember that.

Besides, even though Nick had kissed her like he'd meant it, he'd also made it clear that he'd had his one arrow and had no intention of ever falling in love again. She was smart enough to know that a kiss had nothing to do with love. Nick could want her in his bed, but he'd told her that his heart was closed for business.

Besides, even if he ever changed his mind about loving again, he was the kind of man who would choose a traditional kind of woman, not a woman like Lexie.

And I'm just here in town until I can find Lauren, she thought. She had a job to return to, an apartment and a life that had nothing to do with Widow Creek.

Unable to sit still another minute, she got up off the sofa and grabbed her car keys. She couldn't just sit around here and do nothing. Deciding to go back into town and ask more people about the last time they'd seen Lauren, she left the house.

The sun was warm as it cast through the autumn-colored leaves of the trees she passed. Both Lexie and

Lauren had always loved fall. It had definitely been their favorite season, but now Lexie couldn't take pleasure in its beauty.

There was a huge lump in her chest that she knew wouldn't go away until she found her sister. *Surely if she were dead I'd know it,* Lexie thought. *Surely being identical twins I'd feel it if she were no longer on this earth.*

Or maybe she just wanted to believe that the twin connection was so strong she would know if Lauren had taken her last breath.

Before Nick had called her that morning she'd once again been on Lauren's computer, checking her sister's bank records. There had been no activity since the previous Sunday night when Lauren had paid some bills online.

Wherever her sister was, she wasn't tapping into any money source. Lauren didn't own a credit card. She was one of those smart people who had refused to succumb to the "buy now, pay later" mentality.

She'd also called the Anna who had left a message on Lauren's answering machine again. Although Lexie had spoken to the woman once before, she felt the need to check again and see if perhaps Lauren had called her about the missed appointment.

Anna Cartwell was a nice, elderly woman who had recently bought a poodle puppy. She'd told Lexie that Precious the puppy had already had one session with Lauren but when she'd shown up for her second session the day before, Lauren hadn't been home. She hadn't heard from Lauren but promised to call Lexie if she did hear from her.

And Lexie promised to let Anna know when Lauren would be available to reschedule an appointment for Precious. She just prayed there would be another appointment with Lauren for the poodle pup.

By the time Lexie parked on Main Street her heart was racing with the need to find something, anything that would lead to her sister.

She got out of her car and decided to once again hit all the stores and talk to the shopkeepers. Maybe there would be different people working than when she and Nick had last asked questions.

She started at one end of the block and it didn't take her long to work her way through all the businesses on that side of the street as she saw the same familiar faces in each place and knew they'd have nothing to give her.

In the feed store across the street an unfamiliar face greeted her as she walked through the door. Before when she and Nick had been here they had spoken to a teenage boy behind the counter.

"Can I help you?" the older woman wearing a Fred's Feed shop apron asked.

"I hope so," Lexie replied. "I'm trying to find out when the last time my sister was seen in town. Lauren Forbes?"

"Ah, I see the resemblance," the woman replied with a smile. "Lauren's a regular customer. Let's see, the last time she was in was last Wednesday, she picked up some doggy vitamins she'd ordered."

"Are you sure it was Wednesday?" Lexie asked in surprise.

"Had to be. I didn't work Tuesday or Thursday of last week and if I remember right she came in just before noon."

"Did she say anything about going out of town or anything like that?"

The woman shook her head. "No, she just picked up what she'd ordered and then left."

Lexie thanked the woman and as she left the store she realized that if Bo had been telling the truth about leaving town on Tuesday night then this news was confirmation that Lauren had been alive and well when he'd left.

So, what had happened to Lauren after she'd left the feed store? She'd apparently made it back home, parked her car in the garage and then what? Had somebody been waiting in the garage for her?

Lexie stood just outside the store on the sidewalk and looked around, but there was nothing in sight to give her a clue as to what might have happened when her sister had left Fred's Feed.

She hadn't heard from Gary Wendall, so she headed toward the police station. She'd almost reached the building when she felt the strange sensation of somebody watching her.

Glancing over her shoulder she saw a tall, dark-haired man leaning against one of the vacant storefronts across the street. Even from the distance between them she could see a livid scar that raked down the left side of his face.

His intent gaze seemed to reach across the distance and the hair on the nape of her neck rose in response. Who was he and why was he staring at her so strangely? It was definitely creeping her out.

She quickened her steps and breathed a sigh of relief as she entered the police station. The receptionist ushered her into the office where Gary sat behind his desk.

"Ms. Forbes," he said as he rose from his chair to greet her.

"Chief Wendall, I was wondering if you had any news for me about my sister."

"Please, have a seat, and call me Gary," he said.

Lexie sank down in the chair opposite his desk and nodded. "And you can call me Lexie," she replied. "Now, about my sister's case…"

"Unfortunately, so far I have nothing to offer you," Gary said as he sat back at his desk. "I've contacted the hospital and checked with the morgue and thankfully she isn't in either of those places. I've got a couple of my men asking questions around town but so far we've come up empty. I figured we'd give it until the end of today and then launch a full-blown investigation."

"Why wait?" Lexie countered. She felt as if every minute was of the essence. In another couple of days it would be a full week that Lauren had been gone.

"If this was a child or a minor missing I'd have my men all over it, but this is a grown woman and there is absolutely no sign of foul play."

"How do you know that?" she asked, trying to keep the edge out of her voice. "You haven't even come out to the house to look around." Lexie was aware that despite her efforts her voice was filled with her frustration. The man was an ass, an incompetent ass at that.

"You told me you were staying out at Lauren's place. I figured if something looked odd there you'd have told me by now. I was planning on bringing a couple of men out later today to take a look around. Will you be there around four this afternoon?"

"I'll make it a point to be there," she replied and stood. There was nothing more here for her. She could only hope that maybe Gary and his men might see something she'd missed at the house, something that would provide some answers. "I'll see you around four at Lauren's," she said.

As she left the office she told herself that Gary was probably doing what any law enforcement man would do in this situation. Just because he hadn't come up with any answers yet didn't mean he was an incompetent ass.

She just wanted somebody beating the bushes, turning over rocks and doing a house-to-house search. She just wanted somebody to find her sister.

As she left the police station she saw the dark-haired man just across the street, and once again he stared at her in a way that made her distinctly uncomfortable.

Who was he? And why did he appear to be watching her? Had he waited for her to come out of the police station? What could he possibly want, and if he wanted something then why didn't he approach her?

She got into her car and pulled away as she checked her rearview mirror. To her surprise she saw the man get into a big, black pickup and follow after her.

As she headed toward Lauren's place she divided her attention between the road and her rearview mirror and the truck behind her. He didn't drive too close to her, but the fact that he was there at all caused a rivulet of anxiety to dredge through her.

Was he the person who had been outside of Lauren's house in the middle of the night? Why had he been staring at her? What did he want from her? His presence felt threatening.

The fear spiked as she drew closer to Lauren's place. She didn't want to go there where she would be all alone and he might follow her into the driveway.

Instead when she reached Nick's driveway she pulled in, hoping that he was home. As she made the turn a glance in her mirror let her know the pickup had zoomed on. She parked in front of the attractive two-story house and breathed a deep sigh of relief as Nick stepped out on his front porch.

She got out of the car, surprised to feel her legs slightly shaky beneath her. "Sorry to bother you," she said as she approached where he stood on the porch. She gave a quick glance back at the road and then looked back at him.

"Problems?" he asked.

"A guy in town kind of freaked me out and when I got into my car to drive home, he followed me. I decided to pull in here instead of going on to Lauren's." She was surprised by how shaky she felt about the whole situation. Although the man hadn't really done anything bad, she'd definitely felt threatened.

"Come on in," he opened the front door and she swept past him and into the foyer of the home.

Almost immediately her feet were attacked by a little black ball of fur. "Taz, no!" Nick said.

"What have we here?" Lexie leaned down and picked up the puppy who then attempted to lavish her face with kisses. Lexie laughed, the fear that had gripped her momentarily impossible to maintain with the wiggling warmth of the affectionate dog in her arms.

"That is the dog from hell," Nick said, but his affection for the little pooch was evident in his voice. "Come on into the kitchen."

She placed the dog on the floor and then followed him through a large living room. Her first impression was of a room rarely used. The furniture was overstuffed and looked comfortable, but there was nothing to give the room a real sense of home.

She followed Nick into a large, airy kitchen, and it was in here she felt his presence. A coffee mug sat on the table along with the morning paper. A handful of pocket change and his keys were on the counter along with several dog treats.

"Have a seat," he said. "Want something to drink?"

She shook her head. "No, I'm fine." She sat at the table and Taz collapsed at her feet, as if he'd completely exhausted himself in his exuberant greeting of her.

Nick sat across from her, his gray eyes narrowed slightly. "So, tell me what happened."

"I think maybe I overreacted," she said, suddenly feeling rather foolish. "I went back into town to see if there was anyone working in the stores who we didn't question before. I found a woman in the feed store that told me Lauren had been in on Wednesday to pick up some supplies."

Nick leaned back in his chair. "So, she was okay after Bo left town on Tuesday night."

"Apparently," Lexie agreed. "Anyway, when I left the feed store I noticed a man standing across the street who seemed to be staring at me."

She felt the hairs at the nape of her neck lift as she remembered him. "Even though it made me uncomfortable, I walked down the street to the sheriff's office because I wanted an update from him on the case. When I came out the same man had moved to stand across the street from the police station and he was staring at me once again. When I got in my car to go back to Lauren's, he jumped in his truck and followed me. I got freaked out and so I pulled in here instead of going home."

There was no way she could explain that for a moment what she'd felt wafting off the man had been something bad...something evil.

A frown had swept over Nick's features and had deepened with each word that she said. "This guy, what did he look like?"

"Tall with big shoulders and dark hair, and he had a scar down one cheek."

"Clay Cole," Nick announced. "He's my age, not married and a pseudo-rancher who lives on the north side of town."

"A pseudo-rancher? What does that mean?" she asked curiously.

"He says he's a rancher and he's got a big spread, but he spends more time in the local bars than he does working his land. That's how he got that scar on his face, in a bar brawl. He got cut up with a broken beer bottle."

"Why would he be staring at me so intently? Why would he follow me?"

Nick shoved back from the table and stood. "Why don't we go ask him?"

Lexie stared up at him in surprise. "You mean go to his house?"

"Why not? I figure if you want answers, go directly to the horse's mouth, so to speak. Clay occasionally gets a snootful of booze and picks fights, but when he's sober he's always been an okay kind of guy."

Lexie got up from the table and once again her legs felt slightly shaky. She'd like to get some answers from Clay Cole, but the idea of confronting him face-to-face sent a small shiver of apprehension through her. She couldn't help feeling that somehow she and Nick were getting deeper into something dangerous...she just wasn't sure what it was.

Chapter Five

What Nick hoped to do by taking her out to Clay's was ease some of the anxiety he felt rolling off her. As they passed Lauren's place he saw her look, maybe hoping to see Lauren standing out by the dog pen or mowing the lawn.

He heard the faint sigh of disappointment that released from her as they passed on by and he wished he could say something to ease her worries.

He liked the idea that she'd felt threatened and had come to his place. It meant she trusted him. He was surprised by how much he wanted her to trust him, to depend on him if she was scared.

"I feel bad taking up so much of your time," she finally said, breaking the silence that had descended between them from the moment they'd gotten into his car.

"Over the last year I've had way too much time on my hands," he replied. It was true, since Danielle's death he'd come precariously close to falling into a depression, into wallowing in self-pity. If nothing else Lexie had forced him to look outside of himself, outside of his own heartache, and no matter what happened between them from here on out he would forever be grateful to her for that.

Unfortunately, he didn't know what had happened to Lauren. He couldn't give her a happy ending where her sister was concerned, and it was a fact that his optimism about finding her alive and well was beginning to fade away.

He could only hope that Lexie was strong enough to survive whatever the future held for her. And if she couldn't be strong enough on her own, then he hoped he could be strong for her.

"What did Gary have to say about the case?" he asked.

A frown of irritation crept across her forehead. "Nothing much. He's got his men asking questions and he'd checked the hospital and morgue. He's supposed to be at Lauren's at around four to take a look around there."

"What's he hope to find?"

She shrugged her slender shoulders. "I don't know. Maybe something I missed. Maybe a clue that I've over-looked." She clenched her fingers together in her lap. "I just want him to be doing something." She flashed him a quick glance. "I want everyone to be doing something to help find her."

How well Nick knew that feeling. "In the days that Danielle was missing I felt as if I was the only person on earth who cared about her, the only person who was worried about her. I've never felt as alone as I did in those three long days."

He glanced at Lexie and she smiled at him, that warm open smile that made his heart do a crazy dance in his chest. "I'd feel like that now if it wasn't for you."

She broke the eye contact and cast her gaze out the side window and once again Nick wished he could say something that would take the sadness out of her eyes.

He had no idea why Clay would have been staring at Lexie enough to make her feel uncomfortable. He couldn't imagine why Clay would have followed her out of town, but he intended to find out. He hadn't forgotten that somebody had been outside of Lauren's place in the middle of the night.

Had it been Clay? And if so, what had he been doing out there? What had he wanted? Nick had known Clay almost all his life, the two had gone to school together from kindergarten to graduation from high school.

Clay wasn't the brightest bulb in the package; he had a reputation for being lazy and liked his beer more than most. But Nick couldn't imagine why he'd have any reason to make Lexie uncomfortable or why he might follow her.

When they pulled up in front of Clay's sad-looking ranch house his truck was parked in the driveway, letting them know he was home.

Nick didn't expect any trouble, but he could feel Lexie's tension as they got out of the car. Clay had definitely spooked her and Nick wanted to know why.

It made no sense and Nick wasn't comfortable with things that didn't make sense.

Clay's house didn't breathe of prosperity, but rather, like many of the businesses in town, gave the impression of just barely hanging on.

The white paint had weathered to a dull gray and wood rot was evident around all of the windows. What had once been dark blue shutters were faded and hung askance.

There were several outbuildings in the distance, a barn that looked as tired as the house and a metal gardening shed that looked fairly new and sturdy.

Clay answered on the second knock and was obviously surprised to see them. "Hey, Nick, what's up?"

"Mind if we come in and speak with you?" Nick asked.

"Course not." Clay opened the screen door to allow them into the house.

Nick had never been inside Clay's home before and he was surprised by the lush living room and all that it contained. A rich leather sofa and recliner chair made the perfect place to sit to watch the flat-screen television, which was the biggest Nick had ever seen.

Several of the latest game systems sat on the floor next to the wall where the television was mounted and a state-of-the-art computer was on a nearby desk. Clay might not be putting any money into the outside of his place, but it was obvious he was spending it for his own entertainment and comfort.

"Clay, this is Lauren Forbes's sister, Lexie," Nick said.

"And I want to know why you were staring at me earlier when I was in town." Lexie said without preamble. *So much for finesse,* Nick thought. Lexie was nothing if not direct.

Clay rocked back on his heels and grinned at her. "You noticed that, huh? To be honest, I ain't never seen nobody with pink hair before. Besides, I think you're kinda cute."

Lexie's cheeks flamed with color and Nick had a sudden impulse to throw his arm around Lexie's shoulder and say, "mine," which was ridiculous. She wasn't *his* and he had no intention of making her his.

"You made her nervous, Clay," he said. "She's here in town looking for her sister."

"And nothing else," Lexie said, a hint of pink lingering on her cheeks.

"Yeah, I heard Lauren had gone missing and you two have been in town asking questions about her," Clay said. "I guess you haven't found her yet?"

"Do you know my sister?" Lexie asked.

"Sure, I've seen her around town," Clay replied. "But I didn't really talk to her or nothing like that. I heard through the grapevine that she was seeing Bo Richards."

Nick nodded. "Yeah, we've talked to Bo, but he doesn't know what happened to her."

Clay shrugged his massive shoulders. "Sorry I can't help you." He looked at Lexie and raised a hand to run a finger down his scar. "And sorry I made you nervous. I didn't know it was a crime to gawk at a pretty lady."

"Well, thanks for your time," Nick said. He could tell that Clay was making Lexie uncomfortable even now and Nick wanted nothing more than to get her out of there. He grabbed Lexie by the arm and drew her back to the door.

"Let me know if I can do anything to help," Clay said.

"Don't hold your breath," Lexie muttered as they walked toward the car.

"He's a piece of work," Nick said to Lexie as he backed out of the driveway.

She nibbled on her lower lip, as if trying to work out something in her mind. "Occasionally I've seen a man look at me with what I thought was interest, but that's definitely not how I felt when Clay looked at me." She turned and gazed at him. "The looks from Clay felt darker, filled with a malevolence of some kind." She released a small, embarrassed laugh. "Maybe I'm going crazy. Maybe I'm just imagining things and starting to see boogeymen everywhere."

Nick started the engine with a smile. "Somehow you don't strike me as the type of woman to go that crazy."

"The ranching business must be really lucrative," she said as Nick pulled away from the house. "Did you see all the toys he had inside?"

"Yeah, I'd like to know how a rancher who never seems to get his hands dirty makes the kind of money to afford all that," Nick replied.

"Maybe he's got family money."

Nick laughed and shook his head. "I knew Clay's parents. His father was a drunk and his mother worked long hours at the café. There's no way there was any big money in that family."

"Maybe he works harder than you think he does."

"Maybe," Nick conceded. There was no way he could know what exactly Clay did to earn money or to judge how he spent what he had. He also couldn't really know just how many hours Clay spent actually working his land.

"The main thing is I never heard Lauren mention anything about Clay. He has no dogs so I can't imagine that they would have interacted in any way."

"If that's the way he comes on to women, then it's no wonder he's single," Lexie said with a touch of disdain. "There's just something a little creepy about him."

"I'm glad that you don't think there's anything creepy about me," he replied. Was he actually flirting with her?

"Nothing creepy that I've noticed yet," she returned with a smile.

"You have plans for dinner?"

"I haven't thought that far ahead," she admitted. "It probably depends on how thorough Gary and his men are at Lauren's house. If they're there late, then I'll just grab a sandwich or something."

He was surprised by the little wave of disappointment that fluttered through him. He wouldn't have minded sharing another meal with her, spending more time with her.

It wasn't like she was an arrow to his heart, he told himself. She was just a distraction from his own loneliness, a woman he enjoyed spending time with for now.

As they started past Lauren's place she sat up straight in the seat. "Turn in," she exclaimed.

He whirled the steering wheel to make the turn into the driveway and saw what had grabbed her attention. Gary Wendall's official car was there, along with several other vehicles.

"He must have decided to come early," she said with a glance at her wristwatch.

As they drew closer Nick felt a tightness spring to his chest. He recognized one of the men who stood next to Wendall. It was Roger Wiley, the town coroner.

There would be only one reason for Roger to be here. *No.* The word whispered inside his brain as he pulled the car to a halt and glanced over at Lexie.

She didn't know Roger but she must have seen something on Gary's grim face for she released a little gasp as she got out of the car. Nick hurried after her, instinctively not wanting her to face the next few minutes alone.

"What's going on?" she asked.

Her voice sounded tight, as if she needed to cough. Nick's heart constricted tight in his chest as he took her hand in his and stared at Gary, dreading what was about to come.

"I'm afraid I have some bad news," he began.

Her hand squeezed Nick's painfully tight. "No." The word was a faint whisper of denial from her lips.

At that moment several officers appeared on the edge of the wooded area in the distance. They stood as if awaiting further orders and it was at that moment that Nick realized they must have found Lauren somewhere in the woods.

Lexie must have noticed the officers as well. "No," she said, this time louder and more firmly, as if by that single word alone she could change the course of fate.

"It looks like she must have slipped on the bank of the stream and hit her head," Gary began.

Before he could say another word Lexie yanked her hand from Nick's and took off running.

LEXIE RACED TOWARD the woods, her heart pounding so fast it ached in her chest and she couldn't catch her breath. It had to be a mistake. It couldn't be Lauren. Gary Wendall was wrong. Somehow, someway he had to be wrong!

Even as those thoughts shot through her brain, tears blurred her vision and denial surged up inside her. *Not Lauren. Oh God, please not Lauren.*

There was no ambulance. If she'd been hurt then shouldn't there have been some emergency vehicles standing by? This thought caused the pressure in her chest to intensify.

She flew by the officers, somehow feeling that if she got to Lauren quickly enough she could make everything okay. She had to make everything okay. Anything else was unacceptable.

However, in the depths of her soul she knew it wasn't

going to be okay. Nothing would ever be okay again. She saw another officer in the distance and she ran toward him, her heart pounding so fast, so loud she could hear nothing else.

Make it be a mistake. Please, make it be a mistake, a voice screamed inside her head. She saw her then, Lauren, on her back on the bank of the little stream. It was obvious she was dead and the grief that sliced through Lexie at the sight of her sister crashed her down to her knees.

A high, keening cry escaped from her as she buried her face in her hands and began to weep. There was nothing else in the world but her grief. She was lost in it, immersed to the point that nothing else mattered, nothing else existed.

Lauren was gone. She would never fulfill all the dreams she'd had. She'd never train her working dogs. She'd never get married and have children.

They'd had a plan, the two of them. Lexie was supposed to be Lauren's maid of honor at her wedding and Lauren was going to be Lexie's. They'd planned it since they were little girls, had talked about how their husbands would have to be best friends and their children would grow up as loving, caring cousins.

Now none of it would happen. Lauren was gone.

And Lexie would never hear her twin's voice again. She'd never have that special close relationship with anyone. She was alone…alone in the world and this thought only made her cry harder.

By the time Nick's hand gently touched her shoulder

her tears were all spent and she was blessedly numb. He pulled her up and into his arms and she stood in his embrace in an endless fog that kept everything at bay.

She had no idea how long they stood together. It seemed like a minute. It seemed like an eternity. "Come on," he finally said softly. "I'll take you back to the house."

Yes, she needed to leave this place. She didn't want to look at her sister again. She didn't want to remember Lauren broken and lifeless.

Like an obedient child she nodded, wanting nothing more than to go to sleep and wake up to realize this had all been a dream, a terrible nightmare, and Lauren was still alive and was going to appear any minute now laughing and joking about the silly trick she'd played on them all.

As they reached the house Wendall approached her, his face somber. "My condolences," he said.

The words meant nothing to her. She had retreated to a place inside her mind where nothing was real, nothing could hurt her. She nodded vaguely to the chief and then Nick took her into the house where Zeus greeted them with a happy bark.

The dogs. Oh God, who was going to love Lauren's dogs? Who was going to take care of them now that Lauren was gone? The grief surged up once again, threatening to bring her out of her cocoon of numbness.

She shoved the thoughts and the emotions away and allowed Nick to lead her into the guest bedroom. Gently he maneuvered her so that she was seated on the edge of the bed. He knelt down and took off her shoes and her only feeling was a vague gratefulness that, at least for now, somebody else was in charge.

He forced her to her feet once again, but only long enough to pull down the covers on the bed. She crawled in and closed her eyes, wanting the sweet escape of sleep. Nick's lips pressed softly against her forehead at the same time he took off her glasses and set them on the nightstand.

"Rest," he whispered and then he was gone.

Gone. Lauren was gone forever. She'd slipped and fallen on the bank of the stream and hit her head. Vaguely Lexie remembered the excruciating pain that had lanced through her skull on the day she'd gotten into her car and decided to drive to Widow Creek.

Had it been at that precise moment that Lauren had fallen, that her spirit had left her body? Had she felt her sister's death and not realized it at the time?

Something niggled at the back of Lexie's brain, something she couldn't quite bring into focus but knew was important. What was it?

She squeezed her eyes more tightly closed and tried to focus on what it was that bothered her, but the gut-wrenching sorrow got in the way. She finally fell asleep and found the sweet oblivion she wanted.

She came awake with a small gasp, her heart pounding furiously. She'd been dreaming and in her dream Lauren had been telling her goodbye and Lexie had been begging her sister not to leave her.

Tears burned at her eyes and she quickly squeezed

them closed again, wanting to reclaim the dream, to have just one more minute with her sister.

But as the last of the dream filtered away and her heartbeat slowed to a more natural rhythm, she knew she wouldn't go back to sleep. The pain of her loss crashed back in. Her heart cried her sister's name. Her grief tasted bitter in the back of her throat and she knew the taste would be with her for a long time to come.

She realized it was quite late. The room was dark and the house was quiet. She rolled over on her side and looked at the illuminated hands on the clock. After one.

Her eyes adjusted to the darkness and she realized she wasn't alone. In the faint moonlight that drifted in through the window she saw Nick asleep in the chair in the corner of the room.

Her heart expanded as she remembered his gentle kiss as she'd drifted off to sleep, as she realized he hadn't left her alone while she'd slept. He'd been right there with her through the dark hours.

She had no idea what kind wind of fate had blown him into her life, but at the moment she was grateful that he was here with her. Unfortunately his presence did nothing to lessen the grief that spiked through her.

She wanted to go back to sleep again and dream of Lauren and this time she wanted to convince her sister not to go. But of course she knew this was a foolish wish that would never come true.

She must have made a noise for Nick's eyes opened, glittering silver in the semidarkness. "Lexie, are you okay?" His voice was soft and filled with a compassion that squeezed the air in her lungs.

"I guess I have to be," she replied as she reluctantly sat up.

"Are you hungry?"

It didn't feel right to think about food, but she had to admit she felt empty inside. "Maybe a little," she finally said.

Nick got out of the chair. "Why don't you come into the kitchen and I'll fix you something to eat?"

"I'll be right in," she replied.

As he left the bedroom Lexie rolled over on her back and stared unseeing at the ceiling. Lauren was gone and all the tears in the world wouldn't bring her back. *Somehow, someway* Lexie was going to have to find the strength to go on all alone.

She got out of the bed, grabbed her glasses from the nightstand and went into the bathroom to wash her face. She stared at her reflection for a long moment. Her eyes were slightly swollen and her hair was slightly lopsided from sleep, but none of those things really entered her mind as she gazed at herself.

Her twin was dead. The person who had kept Lexie centered, the person who had defined her was gone. For a moment the woman in the mirror appeared to be a stranger. Who was she without her twin?

She washed her face and raked her fingers through her hair and then left the bathroom and headed for the kitchen.

Nick stood at the stove in his stocking feet. Several

strips of bacon were beginning to sizzle in a skillet. He gestured her toward the table. "Sit and tell me that you don't hate cheese omelets."

"I don't hate cheese omelets," she repeated dutifully. She eased down at the table, finding it hard to breathe.

"This should all be ready in just few minutes."

She frowned. "I feel guilty even thinking about food right now."

"I know, but you have to eat. Grief doesn't fill you up. Trust me, I know." He flipped the slices of bacon and moved to the refrigerator.

She remembered his own personal tragedy and knew he probably understood the emotions that simmered just beneath the surface in her, emotions she didn't want to tap into because she knew they'd only make everything worse. Lauren would want her to be strong, and some-how, someway she had to find the strength to move ahead.

"Where did they take her?" she asked.

"Forrester's Funeral Home in town." Nick cracked a couple of eggs in a bowl. "You have a lot of decisions to make in the next couple of days."

"I know," she replied and stifled the deep sigh of grief that tried to escape from her. They were deci-sions she didn't even want to think about right now. She already knew that Lauren's will indicated that she left all her worldly possessions to Lexie, as Lexie's did to Lauren. The two sisters had gone to an attorney's office to have the official documents drawn up a year ago.

Tomorrow would be soon enough to think of all the

things that needed to be done. The last things she would ever do for her sister in this lifetime.

She watched as he took up the bacon and then scrambled the eggs in a bowl for the omelet. He moved with the ease of a man comfortable in the kitchen. And why wouldn't he be? For the past year he'd been alone, cooking his own meals, consoling himself when he was sad.

He'd been where she was and she found that thought oddly comforting. He'd survived his tragedy and she'd survive this, too. She'd survive for the sister she'd loved.

When he set the plate in front of her any appetite she thought she might have had was gone. "Eat," he commanded firmly as he sat in the chair next to hers. "The days ahead are going to be difficult ones. You have to eat to keep up your strength."

Dutifully she picked up the fork and forced herself to tackle the omelet. "She'll want to be buried here," she said between bites. "Even though she'd only lived here four months she felt like this was home."

"The Widow Creek Cemetery is a beautiful place," he said softly. "It's where Danielle and my daughter are buried."

"Do you visit their graves often?" she asked curiously. It was so much easier to focus on his tragedy instead of her own.

"Occasionally. Danielle refused to go to our baby's grave but I went by myself a lot during the first few months after we lost her. And after Danielle's death, I visited the cemetery every day for the first couple of months." He frowned. "I think I believed that if I spent

enough time there eventually I'd come to understand
what happened, what went so wrong."

"And did you?"

He gave her a sad smile and shook his head. "No,
and after those couple of months I realized I had two
choices. I could crawl right into that grave with her or
I could get back to the business of living. Needless to
say, I decided to go on living."

Lexie looked down at her plate, surprised to realize
she'd eaten everything on it. She looked back at Nick
and a deep gratitude swept through her. "Thank you for
not leaving me alone."

He reached across the table and his big hand engulfed
hers, warming some of the cold spots she had inside.
"There's no way I'd leave you alone, Lexie. I know what
it's like to be alone with grief and I don't want that for
you."

As she looked into his soft gray eyes, she wanted
him. She wanted the warmth of his body wrapped
around hers. She needed him to keep the horror at bay.

"Come to bed with me, Nick. Come to bed and make
love to me."

His eyes flared wide at her words. "Lexie, that's
probably not a good idea tonight. You're grieving and
you aren't thinking straight and the last thing I'd want
to do is take advantage of you."

"You wouldn't be. I know you've already had your
Cupid's arrow, Nick. This isn't about love, it's about
need." She got up from the table. "I need to be held. I
need to feel alive. I need you, Nick."

She turned and left the kitchen, knowing with a woman's instinct that he would follow, knowing he would give her what she needed. He would never marry her and he would never be in love with her, but he did desire her. She'd tasted his desire in the single kiss they had shared. She'd seen it occasionally sparkling in his eyes over the last two days.

When she got to the bedroom she didn't hesitate. Once again she felt as if she'd been wrapped in a layer of cotton that numbed all of her senses.

She'd just taken off her T-shirt when Nick appeared in the doorway and her need to be held, to feel something other than the wild grief that simmered just beneath the surface, raced through her.

He remained in the doorway, as if afraid to cross the threshold into the bedroom. As she stepped out of her jeans and then took her glasses off and set them on the nightstand she felt no shame about what she was about to do.

She was going into this with her eyes open, knowing that what they were about to share had nothing to do with promises or forever, it was just something to get her through the agonizingly long night.

When she was clad only in her bra and panties, she walked over to where he stood, opened her arms to him and whispered his name. He came to her then and wrapped her in his arms.

Closing her eyes, she reveled in the strength his arms contained, the warmth of their bodies together that shot through her and stole away an edge of the numbness.

He held her close enough that she could feel that he was aroused and she knew she hadn't been wrong about him desiring her. He might not be hers for forever, but he could be hers for the night. And at the moment that was more than enough for her.

His lips warmed her forehead in a surprisingly chaste kiss. "Go to bed, Lexie," he said in a soft voice. "Get a good night's sleep."

She raised her face to look at him. "I don't want to sleep. I want you. Don't worry, my mind isn't fuzzy with grief. I know exactly what I'm doing and I know exactly what I want."

She took a small step back from him and began to unbutton his shirt. He stood frozen, with all of his muscles tensed, but he didn't stop her. When his shirt was unfastened she pushed it off his broad shoulders and that seemed to snap the inertia that had gripped him.

This time when his lips found her, they took her mouth with a fiery intent that stole her breath away. She wrapped her arms around his neck and pulled him close…closer still.

His tongue tasted hers and she nipped at his lower lip. She didn't want tenderness, rather she wanted wild and abandoned, hard and frenzied, mind-numbing sex.

She broke the kiss and reached behind her and unfastened her bra. It fell to the floor and she turned and slid into the bed. In the moonlight she watched as he took off his pants and then, clad only in a pair of black boxers and his dark socks, he froze by the side of the bed.

"I don't have protection," he said.

"I'm on the Pill," she replied. "I don't sleep around, Nick, and I know you don't either. I trust you if you trust me." There was no worry in her mind as he, too, slid beneath the sheets and once again took her in his arms.

His mouth found hers in a kiss that sparked her numb senses to life. She wanted to lose herself in him, forget the day that had passed and not think about the days to come. She wanted just this moment to exist.

His mouth left hers and blazed a trail of fire down her throat as his hands covered her bare breasts. Her nipples tightened and rose in response to the heat of his hands and she closed her eyes and gave herself to the sweet sensations his touch evoked.

When his mouth covered one of her nipples she tangled her hands in his hair. His tongue lightly flicked the taut bud and she wanted more, wanted harder, needed faster.

Reaching her hand between them, she stroked the hard length of him on top of his boxers and then plucked impatiently at the material.

"Slow, Lexie," he whispered against her breast.

"I don't want slow," she protested.

He raised his head and looked at her, his eyes pools of glitter. She sensed his smile rather than saw it. "I know exactly what you want, exactly what you need. Believe me, we're going to get there…eventually."

His words shot a new wildness through her. She rolled away from him and tore off her panties, unwilling to wait for eventually.

But he remained in control, stroking her body in slow, languid caresses that made her want to scream for release. His hands seemed to be everywhere, whispering the length of her body, lingering on her inner thigh and smoothing across the flat of her lower stomach.

He seemed determined to keep her mindless with need, lingering in a state of limbo of trembling desire without fulfillment.

Finally his fingers found the center of her and as he touched her there she gasped and moaned his name. There was no thoughts of anything but him and the sweet sensations that rushed through her. When he began to apply pressure, she arched to meet him as she felt the rush of her release. And then it was on her, trembling through her with a force that left her breathless.

It was only then that he kicked off his boxers and moved on top of her. She grabbed his buttocks as he entered her, but he refused to move his hips. Instead he remained still except for dipping his head down to capture her lips in a tender kiss.

As the kiss ended she released a half sob, half moan and he began to thrust into her. She loved the feel of him, both his skin against hers and the way he filled her up so completely.

He gave her fast and furious and he gave her slow

and tender and she was lost in him, breathing him in as he took possession of her.

He kissed her so hard he growled into her mouth and then moved his lips like butterfly wings against hers. The hard and fast followed by the tender and slow sent her spiraling again and this time when she came he moaned her name as his own release shuddered through him.

He sagged against her, their breaths coming in quick gasps that finally began to slow. He softly whispered her name as he pulled her close against him. And when their heartbeats were back to normal, when the rush of the release waned, tears burned once again at Lexie's eyes.

The tears weren't just for her sister, but also because she knew Nick was a one arrow man and he'd had his great love. The tears were because no matter what she and Nick had just shared, no matter how wonderful it had been, ultimately Lexie was all alone in the world.

Chapter Six

It was a gray, cloudy morning as Nick sat at Lauren's kitchen table and sipped from a cup of coffee. He stared out the window and absently watched the chilly autumn wind whip the trees and leaves flutter to the ground amid the assault.

However, his thoughts weren't on the turn in the weather, but rather on the woman who still slept in the bedroom. He had no illusions about what had happened the night before. She hadn't come at him with love or any real passion, but rather with a frantic need to keep her grief at bay.

He'd been in her shoes. In the days and weeks after Danielle's death he'd wanted to lose himself, to find some sort of oblivion that would take the bitter taste of grief out of his mouth. For about a week after Danielle's death he'd found his escape in the bottom of a bottle, and he knew last night Lexie had found hers, at least for a brief time, in his arms.

He frowned and took another drink from the mug. There were a million things he should be doing at the moment. Although Taz was proficient at using the doggy door to go out in the dog run to do his business, there was no telling what the little rascal had found to tear up while Nick had been gone.

There were morning chores to do and yet he felt as if the most important chore he had was to be here for Lexie. He knew when she woke up the jagged edges of her grief would be with her once again, poking and prodding and making her half-crazy with loss. He didn't want her to be alone.

Or was it possible that *he* didn't want to be alone?

He shoved this disturbing thought out of his head. This wasn't about him. He knew there were any number of women in town who would be happy to keep him company. Since Danielle's death several of the single women in town had come on to him with a vengeance, but none of them had touched him like Lexie.

She was getting to him in a way nobody had since Danielle. He didn't want to do it again. He didn't want a woman depending on him for anything. He didn't want to try again. He couldn't stand the idea of failing again.

Of course, it was just a matter of days now and Lexie would be gone. Once Lauren had been buried there was nothing to keep her here.

He'd just refilled his coffee cup and sat down again in the chair when Lexie came into the room. She'd apparently showered and dressed for the day in a pair of jeans and a long-sleeved pink knit blouse.

She wore her grief like an open wound on her face. Behind her thick-rimmed glasses her eyes were swollen and her face was lined as if she hadn't slept for days.

She nodded to him and went directly to the coffee-maker on the counter. He said nothing, deciding to let her take the lead. She didn't speak until she had her coffee and was seated across from him at the table.

"If I wasn't such a selfish person I would insist that you go home," she said as she raised her cup to her lips. "I'm sure you have plenty of things to take care of there."

"I do," he admitted. "But I thought maybe after you have your coffee we could head over to my place for breakfast and I can take care of some of the morning chores."

"Or I could just stay here and let you get on with your life." She took a sip of her coffee and eyed him cautiously over the rim of the cup.

"Is that what you want?" he asked.

"Not really." She lowered her cup back to the table with a sigh. "I just don't feel like being alone right now."

"And I don't intend to leave you alone."

She picked up her cup and took another sip, and when she finished she tilted her head to the side and held his gaze. "I can't imagine why Lauren wasn't madly in love with you. You're handsome and smart and such a nice man."

He smiled, ridiculously pleased by the compliments. "There's no accounting for chemistry between two people. There just weren't any romantic sparks between me and Lauren. Besides, Lauren knew the score. She knew I wasn't looking for anyone in my life." He wasn't sure if that was a reminder to Lexie or a reminder to himself that he was unavailable for love.

She nodded and cast her gaze out the window. "Looks like rain," she said.

"Yeah, according to the weather report I heard this morning it's supposed to rain off and on over the next couple of days." The weather would only make things more difficult for her, he thought. Dismal and cold only added another layer of pain to somebody suffering from grief.

She finished her coffee and got up to carry her cup to the sink. "Whenever you're ready to go to your place, I'm ready."

Within minutes they were in his car and headed to his house. Lexie was quiet and he didn't attempt to engage her in conversation.

He knew there were no words he could give her that would take away the pain of her loss. It was only recently that his ache of loss over Danielle had diminished to a manageable level.

When they reached his place Taz greeted them at the door with a happy dance around their feet. For the first time in the past twenty-four hours a smile danced across Lexie's face as she picked up the squirming dog.

"Hey, little guy," she said as she hugged him close to her chest. Taz responded by licking the underside of her chin with enthusiasm.

"Make yourself at home," Nick said. "I'm going to head out to the barn and get some things taken care of."

"I'll be fine," she assured him.

Eventually she would be fine, he thought as he headed out of the house. She'd bury her sister and then get back to her life in Kansas City. Eventually he and Widow Creek would be just a distant memory that she only revisited occasionally in her mind. He was surprised that this thought made him sad.

It took him over an hour to finish up his chores. Nick kept a herd of cattle in the pastures beyond the barn, but he also had several horses and needed to check their water supply and feed. Most of his money came from the cattle and crops he grew in other pastures. Still, there were always things that needed to be done to keep the place running smoothly. When he returned to the house he found Lexie on the sofa with a sleeping Taz in her lap.

She smiled as he entered. "He finally wore himself out," she said.

"Tell the truth, he finally wore you down," Nick replied.

"Maybe a little of both." Her smile fell. "I need to figure out what I'm going to do with Lauren's dogs."

He sat on the sofa next to her. "There are several other dog breeders in the area. Maybe we can contact them and one of them will be interested in taking the dogs."

She nodded. "All of them except Zeus. I'm not sure what I'll do with him, but I definitely don't want him going to a stranger."

"I could take him," Nick offered. "He likes me and

I have plenty of room for him. Besides, maybe he can teach Taz some good manners."

Gratitude filled Lexie. If she did take the old dog herself she'd have a problem with the landlord, as she lived in a no-pets apartment. She would have had to find a new place to live that allowed pets.

It felt right for Nick to have Zeus. She knew Zeus would be happy here. "Thanks," she said simply.

He nodded. "And I'll place some calls about the other dogs and see if we can find them a good home. Now, are you ready for something to eat?"

They ate breakfast at Nick's, and then returned to Lauren's house. Lexie got on the phone to the funeral home to make the necessary arrangements for Lauren and Nick used his cell phone to make calls to the local dog breeders in the area.

Lauren's funeral had been arranged for Wednesday morning and on Thursday a breeder from a nearby town was coming out to look at the dogs.

With the business taken care of, Lexie sat at the table and stared out at the woods where her sister had been found. Nick sat across from her, wishing he could think of something to take her sorrow away. But he knew that nothing in the world he could come up with could sweep that emotion away from her. It was going to take time for Lexie to heal from this. Hell, it had been a year since Danielle had been found in that motel room and there were still days when the pain felt fresh.

"I want to take a walk," she said suddenly.

"A walk? A walk where?" he asked curiously.

She pointed toward the woods. "There."

"Oh, Lexie, honey, I don't think that's such a good idea," he protested. Aside from the fact that it was a miserable day, nothing good could come from her walking the area where her sister had tragically died.

Her chin thrust forward. "It's something I need to do, Nick." A frown swooped across her forehead. "I can't tell you why, but I need to go there. Something's bothering me. I'm just not sure what it is yet."

Nick stifled a sigh. He couldn't imagine what it was that was bothering her, and the scene of Lauren's death could only upset her even more. "You sure you don't want to wait until another day?" he asked.

"I want to do it now," she replied.

"If that's what you feel like you need to do then let's take a walk," he finally said, deciding he probably couldn't talk her out of it anyway.

"When we drove in here yesterday and saw all the men—I feel like everything after that happened in a fog," she said as they pulled on jackets and stepped out the back door.

Maybe she needed to go back to assure herself that it was all real, that all the tragedy of the day before had really happened, Nick thought.

"It was a rough day, Lexie," he replied. "Probably one of the worst you'll ever experience in your entire life."

"I know," she replied.

The dead leaves crunched beneath their feet and he sensed Lexie pulling into herself, preparing for the scene of her sister's accident. The sky overhead had grown darker as the day had gone on, as if reflecting Lexie's grief in the gathering dark clouds.

There was a fine mist in the air, as if the clouds hadn't decided yet whether to move on or release a torrent of rain. Nick just wanted for Lexie to do whatever it was she needed to do quickly so both of them could get in before the rain began in earnest.

As they drew closer to the thick grove of trees, her footsteps slowed as if dread was weighing her down. "You don't have to do this, Lexie," he said softly.

"No, I have to," she replied firmly. She stopped and looked at him in obvious confusion. "Something is bothering me. It's been bothering since Lauren was found. I swear Friday evening when I got here and couldn't find Lauren, Zeus and I went completely through these woods."

She broke eye contact with him and looked forward, a frown cutting a vertical line down her forehead. "I told you that everything was a blur yesterday. You need to show me exactly where Lauren was found."

Now she had him curious. "This way," he said and together they began walking again. When they reached the trees he led her along the creek to a rocky area and pointed to the opposite side of the bank. "She was there." He tried not to remember the agonizing cries that had come from Lexie when she'd seen her sister.

Lexie stood frozen and followed the direction of his finger with her gaze. For a long moment she didn't even appear to be breathing as she concentrated on the place where her sister had died.

"She couldn't have been there," she finally said. She reached out and grabbed him by the arm. "Are you sure? Are you positive that it was that exact spot?" Her fingers clenched tight, biting through the material of his lightweight jacket sleeve.

Nick frowned and looked around the area, wanting to be sure of what he was telling her before he spoke again. "Positive," he finally replied. "I remember that fallen tree branch up ahead. She was right there." He looked at Lexie once again. "Why? What's wrong?"

She dropped her hand from his arm. "I sat right there." She pointed down the creek bed, her eyes narrowed behind her glasses. "I sat right on that big rock with Zeus next to me the first night I got here."

She took several steps forward, her body vibrating with barely suppressed energy. "We would have seen her if she'd been there. Zeus would have found her or at least would have sensed her presence in the area. I knew something was bothering me last night before I went to sleep, but I couldn't put my finger on it. That's what was bothering me. Lauren couldn't have slipped and fallen the way they said she did at the time they said she did. If she had I would have found her Friday night."

Nick walked to her side and looked at her in confusion. "What are you saying, Lexie?"

She stared at him with those big, beautiful eyes. "I'm saying that she must have been killed and then moved here to make it look like an accident. I'm saying that my sister was murdered."

She didn't wait for his response but instead turned and headed back to the house.

LEXIE FELT AS IF SHE WERE on fire as she headed back to the house. Her brain screamed with troubling thoughts that shifted around and around like nebulous shadows, seeking some kind of logical explanation for what didn't make sense.

She was vaguely aware of Nick following behind her as she entered the house, yanked off her jacket and then stood in the center of the kitchen, unsure of what she should do next.

"Lexie, sit down," Nick said as he took off his own jacket. "Tell me what's going on in your head."

She looked at him helplessly, then sank down at the table. He sat next to her, the familiar scent of him momentarily slicing through the chaos in her mind.

If she hadn't been in such a fog of grief the evening before when Lauren had first been found she would have realized that something was wrong...something was very wrong about the whole situation.

Nick's gray eyes gazed at her in confusion and for just a moment she wanted to fall into their depths, lose herself once again in the warmth and comfort of his arms and forget the bad feeling that now threatened to embrace her.

She shoved that desire away, knowing that it was

just a convenient and very temporary escape from the questions that now clawed at her.

"There's no way that sometime on Wednesday or Thursday Lauren fell and hit her head and died there on that creek bank, because if she had I would have found her body there Friday night. I think Lauren was killed someplace else and then moved there." She wondered if he thought her grief was making her crazy.

"Nick, I'm telling you she wasn't there Friday night. I walked that entire area. Zeus and I searched for her. She wasn't there and nobody can make me believe otherwise."

He frowned. "But if what you say is true, then Gary Wendall would have had to know about it, he'd have to be a part of it. Gary is lazy and maybe more than a little incompetent, but I can't imagine that he'd kill a woman or know somebody who did and then conspire to make her death look like an accident. And in any case why would he or anyone else want Lauren dead?"

Lexie blew out a sigh. "I don't know." She took off her glasses and rubbed at her eyes, wondering if her grief was, indeed, making her crazy. Who on earth would want to harm her sister? Lauren had been kind and generous and Lexie couldn't remember anyone ever having a beef of any kind with her.

"If you really believe that, then what do you intend to do about it?" he asked.

"The first thing I'm going to do is get back in touch with the funeral home and tell them I want a complete autopsy on Lauren. I want to know if the head wound that killed her was from a slip and fall or from blunt force trauma."

"And if you find out it was blunt force trauma?"

A well of strength rose up inside her, strength born from the love of her sister. "Then I'll find out who is responsible for killing my sister and I'll make them pay for their crime." It was a promise not just to herself but to Lauren.

Unfortunately the call to the funeral home was too late. Lauren had already been embalmed and her wounds cleaned up in a way that would remove any evidence they might have gained from an autopsy.

Lexie was bitterly disappointed at the news, knowing that the best evidence of foul play had been washed away. She decided not to speak to Sheriff Wendall about her suspicions, at least not yet.

For one thing, she wasn't sure what she believed, and in any case she didn't want to give him a heads-up that she had any doubts about how Lauren had died.

But for the next two rainy days the doubts only grew bigger. If Lauren had died an accidental death, then why was her body moved to the creek bed? Lexie would swear under oath that Lauren hadn't been there on the night she and Zeus had walked the property. So, who had placed her there after death?

The rain that had poured down had washed away any evidence that might have been left at the scene. Footprints would be gone, as would any blood spatter pattern there that might prove or disprove Lauren's fall.

During those two days Nick scarcely left her alone.

They spent their hours together talking about theories that made no sense, grieving for Lauren and discussing their lives before they'd met.

Nick talked a little bit about Danielle, who had been the president of their high school student council and a cheerleader.

Lexie found herself telling him about Michael the rat, although she certainly didn't confess to him the hurtful things Michael had said to her when he'd broken up with her.

Each night Lexie insisted Nick go home while she remained at Lauren's. Making love with Nick had been wonderful and Lexie knew if they stayed under one roof for the night it would happen again and she couldn't let that happen.

It would only make things more difficult for her when she left, and eventually she would go back to her home, back to her life.

Nick had heartbreak written all over him and her heart was already shattered enough by Lauren's death. He'd told her he wasn't looking for love again in his life, but even if he was she knew he'd choose some pretty blonde who didn't have a pink streak in her hair, somebody who was socially more adept than Lexie would ever be.

Michael had made it clear to Lexie that she lacked in areas that would make her a companion, a lover for life, and it was a lesson she'd never forgotten.

The morning of Lauren's funeral the sun finally reappeared and shone brilliantly. Lexie stood at the kitchen window sipping coffee with her head filled with thoughts of her sister.

She remembered the two of them playing as children, how supportive Lauren had been in high school when Lexie couldn't find a place where she belonged. Lauren had always tried to include Lexie in her group of friends, had encouraged Lexie to break out of her shyness and make friends of her own.

Bits and pieces of lives shared fluttered through Lexie's mind, alternately filling her with both happiness and tears of sorrow.

While she knew her grief would be with her for a very long time, over the past two days a resignation had slowly washed over her, a weary acceptance that Lauren was truly gone.

But along with the grief she had a fierce determination burning in her soul, the determination to somehow find out the truth about Lauren's death. If somebody had killed her, then Lexie wanted that person in prison for the rest of his or her life.

A knock on her door let her know Nick had arrived to take her to the graveside service she'd arranged. He looked amazingly handsome in a black suit and white shirt, and the first thing he did when he stepped through the door was take her in his arms and wrap her in a bear hug.

She closed her eyes and allowed the warmth of him to invade her soul.

What was she going to do when it was time to leave Widow Creek? Time to leave Nick? She didn't even want to think about that right now. He'd become her staff to lean on, her anchor in a storm-tossed sea. Eventually she'd have to regain her strength and stop depending on him, but at least for today she was grateful to have him by her side.

"You ready for this?" he asked when he finally released her. "It's going to be a tough day."

"I know. I guess I'm as ready as I can be under the circumstances," she replied.

"You look nice," he observed.

"Thanks." She nervously smoothed a hand down the thighs of her black slacks and was grateful she'd packed a black-and-white blouse to go with them. She checked her wristwatch. "I guess we should probably go."

"It's about that time," he agreed. She grabbed her purse and together they left the house.

As she slid into the passenger seat she hoped that along with saying goodbye to Lauren at the funeral she'd get some answers as to who might be responsible for her murder.

Widow Creek might be Nick's hometown, but Lexie believed that at the moment the small town was hiding a murderer and she was determined to do anything in her power to bring that person out in the open.

Chapter Seven

"I don't imagine there will be too many people there," she said as Nick pulled his car out of the driveway and onto the road that led into town. "Lauren wasn't here long enough to make a lot of friends."

"At least the sun is shining," he replied. "It rained something fierce on the day I buried Danielle. It was like the sky cried all the tears that I couldn't release."

She glanced over at him. "I hope this doesn't bring back too many painful memories of that day for you."

He cast her a warm smile. "I'll be fine, Lexie. I'm just here to help you get through a tough day."

And it was a tough day. Lexie was surprised by the amount of people who came to pay their respects. She was also surprised to discover that the tears she'd shed on the night that Lauren's body had been found hadn't been the only ones she had to release.

As the minister spoke of the sorrow of the people of Widow Creek who hadn't gotten the opportunity to know Lauren, to share in her life, deep sobs escaped from Lexie as she was reminded of all the things she'd never share with her twin sister.

Nick kept an arm firmly around her shoulder and she leaned weakly into him as she said her final good-bye to her twin. When the service was over and the crowd began to disperse, Lexie tensed as Gary Wendall ambled up to her and Nick.

"It was a nice service," he said as he pulled his hat off his head. "It was good to see so many people turn out."

"Yes, even though my sister was here only a short time, it appears she made some friends," Lexie replied around the lump in her throat.

Gary put his hat back on his head and rocked back on his heels. "I suppose you'll be heading back to Kansas City now that this is all said and done."

"On the contrary, I have no intention of going any-where until I find out who killed my sister." Lexie hadn't meant to tell him what was on her mind, but as she blurted out the words she watched Gary's face carefully.

His eyes narrowed slightly. "What are you talking about?"

"Somebody whacked my sister over the head and then put her body on that creek bed sometime between the time I arrived at the ranch and when you found her body. I'm not leaving Widow Creek until I have some answers."

Gary flicked a derisive glance to Nick. "You've obvi-ously been spending too much time with him. I hope you two are very happy with your conspiracy theories, but there was nothing to indicate that anyone murdered your sister." Gary released a deep sigh. "Look, Miss Forbes, grief does terrible things to people. If I thought for one minute this was anything other than a tragic accident, I'd be conducting a full-blown investigation. Go home, Lexie. Go home and get on with your life and let your sister rest in peace." He didn't wait for Lexie's response, but instead turned on his heels and headed to his car parked in the distance.

"Come on, let's head back to Lauren's," Nick said.

"You want to visit Danielle and your daughter's graves while we're here?" she asked.

"No, I'm good," he replied and wrapped an arm around her shoulder. "Let's just get out of here."

"You said that in the first few days after Danielle was found you didn't believe that she'd committed suicide," Lexie said when they were back in Nick's car.

"That's right," Nick agreed. "I was definitely into conspiracy theories then. I wondered if somebody had kidnapped Danielle, taken her to that motel, killed her and then staged the scene to make it look like a suicide."

"Odd, isn't it? That two women went missing and have died in strange circumstances and the people closest to them believe both of their death scenes were staged."

Nick shot her a quick glance. "Odd, yes, but I can't imagine how we could possibly tie Lauren's death to Danielle's in any way. Danielle died long before Lauren even moved to town. One worked for the mayor's office and the other was a dog breeder. Trying to connect the two is definitely an impossible stretch."

Unless they'd both run into the same killer, she thought, but she didn't say the thought aloud. Instead she nodded and looked out the passenger window thoughtfully. "I can't figure out if Gary Wendall is a good guy or a bad guy."

"I've never thought of him as a bad guy. Lazy, yes, but definitely not bad. You know, if what you think is true about Lauren, it's possible that Gary knows nothing about it, that her body was moved there by somebody else altogether before he and his men showed up. Maybe the shadow man you saw in the night is responsible."

The shadow man. Lexie's stomach muscles clenched tight. It was as good as any description for the person she'd thought had been on Lauren's property. Had it been at that moment that he'd been moving Lauren's body to the creek bed, the night that the dogs had gone crazy?

How she wished she would have grabbed her gun and left the house. How she wished she would have gone outside to investigate. She might have come face-to-face with the person who had killed her sister. *And you might have been killed, too,* a little voice whispered.

Nick turned into Lauren's driveway. "In any case, you're probably going to be too busy for the rest of the day to think much about anything."

She looked at him in surprise. "Why?"

"If I know this town there are two things that bring everyone all together, the fall festival and death. Trust me, by the time this evening comes you're going to have a lot of company and more food in the house than you could eat in a month."

He was right. Within an hour, people began to arrive, bringing with them condolences and covered dishes.

Lexie was overwhelmed by the people and the food that kept coming throughout the afternoon. She found herself staying close to Nick, depending on him to introduce the people she hadn't met and to aid her in the social interactions she'd always found difficult.

Lexie met the woman who had trimmed Lauren's hair while she'd been living here and Anna, who had been bringing her poodle for obedience lesions. The man who'd fixed the brakes on Lauren's car a month before introduced himself and then self-consciously drifted away.

Lexie couldn't help but look at each person with an edge of suspicion at the same time she fought the grief that bubbled far too near the surface.

Bo Richards showed up, his sorrow evident on his handsome features as he first shook Nick's hand and then smiled sadly at Lexie. "I wish I would have taken your sister with me to meet my parents," he said to Lexie. "If she'd gone with me then maybe this horrible thing wouldn't have happened to her."

"We can't know that for sure," Lexie replied. But, armed with the belief that her sister had been murdered, she continued to watch Bo as he walked away and disappeared into the throng of people in the kitchen.

Had he left town on Tuesday night only to return the next day or night, kill Lauren and then return to his parents' home? Was it possible he'd wanted more from Lauren than she'd been willing to give? Or had Lauren wanted to take their relationship to the next level and Bo had grown tired of her?

As far as Lexie was concerned everyone was a suspect, everyone except Nick. He was the only person she trusted in this godforsaken town.

It was growing dark outside when a middle-aged man in a well-cut suit approached her. "Ms. Forbes, I'm Vincent Caldwell, the mayor of Widow Creek." He took Lexie's hand in his. "I just wanted to tell you how very sorry I am about what happened to your sister. I know she would have been a vital part of this little town had this tragedy not happened."

His eyes were a warm blue and as he squeezed her hand sympathetically, Lexie once again felt the burn of tears in her eyes.

Nick was right there beside her, swooping an arm around her shoulder in obvious support. "Vincent, thanks for coming," he said to the mayor. "What's made this even more difficult for Lexie is that we have some doubts as to what really happened to Lauren to cause her death."

Vincent released Lexie's hand and frowned. "What do you mean you have some doubts? I understood that this was a slip and fall, an accidental death." He looked at Nick and then back to Lexie. "Is there something I haven't been told about all this?"

"I think she was killed somewhere else and then

moved to the place where her body was discovered," Lexie replied.

The mayor looked stunned. "Why would you think that?"

Lexie quickly explained about her searching the area on the night she'd arrived in Widow Creek and the fact that Lauren's body had not been there on that night. As she talked, the frown on the mayor's face grew deeper and deeper.

"Have you spoken to Gary Wendall about your concerns?" he asked when she was finished.

"He seems to think we've lost our minds," Nick replied, his voice laced with a touch of irritation.

"I'll talk to him. I certainly don't want a visitor to our town going away with these kinds of questions in her head." He smiled sympathetically at Lexie. "I'll certainly be in touch, Ms. Forbes."

By the time everyone had left Lexie felt totally wrung out. She and Nick worked side by side, wrapping up the leftover food and placing it in the refrigerator.

"You have enough green bean casseroles to feed a group of Pilgrims Thanksgiving dinner," he said as he put the last dish away.

"And I don't even like green bean casserole," she said. "Still, it was nice. So many people came. None of them knew me and a lot of them didn't really know Lauren, but they came out with food and sympathy."

"This town is dying a slow death, but it's not because of the heart of the people," Nick replied. "How about I make us some coffee and we sit in the living room for a little while before you send me home."

"That sounds good," she agreed, needing a little while to just chill before calling it a night. Minutes later Zeus followed them as they left the kitchen and carried their coffee into the living room.

Lexie sat on the sofa and Nick eased down in the nearby chair with Zeus at his feet. Lexie sipped her coffee and then set the mug on the coffee table and released a tired sigh.

"I hope this woman coming tomorrow wants to take the dogs," she said. "I want them to all find good homes."

"From what she told me on the phone she works with several animal rescue organizations so I have a good feeling about it," Nick replied. "Besides, the dogs are young and that's an advantage when it comes to placing them in a home."

Lexie reached for her coffee cup and cradled the warmth in her hands. "Maybe I'm wrong," she said softly.

"Wrong about what?" Nick looked at her in confusion.

"About Lauren being murdered, about her body being moved, about all of it. Maybe I didn't check that particular area of the creek. Maybe I'm just really confused." She'd gone over it and again in her mind and she was no longer sure what she believed anymore.

"What's changed your mind?"

"I don't know. I've just been thinking that maybe I've

been suffering the same ailment that struck you when Danielle died, an overpowering denial and the need to make sense of a terrible tragedy."

She took another sip of her coffee. "Besides, if there was a crime committed, there's almost always a motive and I just can't come up with one in this case. I looked at every single person who showed up today and they all looked guilty to me."

"Even Anna with her poodle Precious?" he asked teasingly.

"She was the only one who didn't set off my radar," Lexie replied. She released a deep sigh. "I think I just have to make peace with the fact that Lauren slipped and fell and when Zeus and I checked the property on Friday night we weren't as thorough as I thought we were."

"I think what you need more than anything is to go to bed. It's been a long day and sleep is the best thing right now." Nick got up from his chair and walked over to Lexie.

Once again she thought about how wonderful it would be to fall into bed with him, to feel his body heat next to hers, to allow his desire to burn away all thought, all heartache, if only for a little while.

"You could stay here tonight with me if you want," she said, her gaze holding his intently.

His eyes flared molten silver as if he knew what she offered wasn't just a bed to sleep in, but rather a bed with her and a night of desire.

He pulled her to her feet and into the warmth of his embrace. At that moment the front window exploded and the sound of gunfire filled the air.

Chapter Eight

Nick yanked Lexie to the floor as bullets smashed through the front window and riddled the opposite wall. Framed pictures crashed to the floor and Zeus barked uncontrollably and then ran out of the living room while Nick covered Lexie's body with his.

His heart beat frantically in his chest as he tried to wrap his brain around what was happening. He was vaguely aware of Lexie screaming beneath him, her shrill cries adding to the cacophony of chaos that surrounded him.

The melee lasted only a minute or two and then Nick heard a squeal of tires from outside and an abrupt silence reigned. He felt Lexie's heart against his own, beating a frantic rhythm of fear.

Her glasses had fallen off and her eyes were wide. "Are you okay?" he asked urgently and became aware of the dogs outside barking raucously.

She nodded. He rolled off her and went to the window, glass crunching underfoot. He looked outside but there was nothing to see. Whoever had made the sudden attack was now gone.

He turned back to look at Lexie and found her on her feet, her glasses back in place. "I changed my mind," she said. "I'm not all right. I'm angry." She brushed off the back of her jeans and then grabbed her purse off the coffee table and pulled out her gun. "I guess maybe somebody isn't happy with the questions I'm asking and wants me to leave town."

She was right. This was either a dangerous warning or somebody had just tried to kill them both. If they hadn't hit the floor when they had there was no question in his mind that one of them might have been seriously wounded or dead.

"We need to call Wendall," he said as she walked to the window to stand next to him.

"You do that," she replied. "And I'm going to stand right here. The next car or truck that pulls in front of this house better be an official patrol car with a cherry on top, otherwise I'm shooting first and asking questions later."

Nick had never seen her this way, so focused, so incredibly strong. Since he'd met her she'd appeared vulnerable and needy but now there was a fire in her eyes that made him realize she was much stronger than he'd initially given her credit for.

As he made the call to Chief Wendall, she remained at the window, not moving, gun pointed out toward the darkness. "Would you find Zeus and make sure he's locked up in a bedroom?" she asked when he'd finished with the call to Wendall. "I don't want him walking around in here and cutting up his paws."

As he went in search of the dog some of the shock of what they'd just been through began to wear off. She was right. Somebody wasn't happy with her...with them. Whether this had been a warning or an attempt to do actual harm, he couldn't know, but one thing was clear—something wasn't right in his hometown and it broke his heart.

He hadn't been sure what to believe about Lauren's death until this moment. All the questions Lexie had had about Lauren's death now seemed credible, not the crazy meanderings of somebody consumed by grief. There was more to Lauren's death that a simple slip and fall.

He found Zeus in the guest bedroom, hunkered down next to the bed. The dog raised his head and whimpered as Nick approached. "It's all right," Nick said as he scratched beneath the old boy's ears. "Everything's going to be fine."

It was easy to make that promise to a cowering dog, but as Nick left the bedroom and closed the door behind him, he wondered what in the hell was going on.

When he returned to the living room Lexie was still in the same position in front of the broken window, her back rigid with tension. "Something is very wrong here," she said.

He picked his way back across the glass-littered rug to stand next to her once again. "I know." The admission was difficult for him. This was his hometown. These were people he thought he knew, people he'd always thought he could trust.

"Any theories?"

"None," he replied. "Maybe now it's time you call in the FBI."

She shook her head. "Right now all we have is a death ruled accidental and a random shooting in a small town, nothing that rises to the standard of FBI involvement."

"At least let Gary know that you're an FBI agent. If nothing else it might shake him up enough to do a more thorough investigation into all this," he replied.

"I'm just not ready to let him know about my job yet. Besides, what I do for a living shouldn't make any difference in how hard he works on his investigation. He should work hard whether I'm an FBI agent or a waitress." She frowned. "If I had some proof that Chief Wendall was dirty, that the local law enforcement agency was corrupt, then I might be able to make a case to get the FBI involved." She straightened her back as the swirling red light on the top of Gary's car came into view. "And it appears the man of the hour has arrived."

"You didn't see the make or model of the vehicle they were driving?" Gary asked minutes later as he surveyed the damage in the living room.

"Unfortunately we were too busy diving for cover," Lexie replied.

"Looks like it was buckshot," Gary observed. "Who have you two managed to stir up?"

"We might have upset Clay Cole," Nick said.

"What did you do to Clay?" Gary asked with a frown.

Nick looked at Lexie, then back at Gary. "Lexie thought he was following her around in town. He made her feel uncomfortable so we went out to his place to have a talk with him. Maybe he took exception to us calling him out."

Gary's frown deepened. "Clay isn't really the type to do something like this. If he has a problem with you he comes at your face in the daylight, not sneaking under the cover of darkness, but I'll certainly check him out. There's also the possibility that it was kids. Last month when old Henry Riley was in the hospital his barn got all shot up and I suspected a couple of kids then."

"Maybe I should contact some of my associates and see if they're willing to come out here and help you with your investigation," Lexie said with a quick glance at Nick.

"Your associates?" Gary looked at her with interest.

"Lexie's an FBI agent," Nick said, oddly satisfied by the stunned surprise on Gary's face.

Gary stared at Lexie. "Is that true?" She nodded and he rocked back on his heels. "Look, this is a local matter, there's no need to get anyone else involved." He took a step closer to Lexie. "I know you feel like I didn't do my job where your sister was concerned, but I did everything in my power under the circumstances. Now I intend to do everything in my power to find out who's responsible for this and what's going on. If after I do my investigative work you still feel like you need to call in somebody else, then by all means do so."

"I just want some answers," Lexie replied. "Why

would somebody do something like this? It's obvious somebody wanted to either warn me or kill me and I want to know why."

"So do I," Gary said grimly. "This is Widow Creek, not Chicago and I won't tolerate drive-by shootings and such nonsense in my town. I've got a couple of kids I want to talk to about this and I'll also talk to Clay. I definitely intend to get to the bottom of things."

Nick wondered if he'd underestimated Gary. He certainly seemed to be taking this issue seriously. "I'm going to take Lexie to my place for the rest of the night," he said and steeled himself for a protest from her, but she said nothing.

"We'll need to board up this window," Gary said and once again looked at Lexie. "I don't want the missing window to be an open invitation for somebody to come in and steal. You know if your sister had any plywood anywhere?"

"I think I remember seeing some in the garage," she replied.

Gary looked at Nick. "Why don't we go take a look and see what we can use."

Together the two men left the house and headed for the garage. "I'm hoping this is just a case of maybe some teenagers who thought the house was empty and decided to have a little fun," Gary said. "But I gotta tell you, Nick. I've got a bad feeling about this."

"That makes three of us," Nick replied as he opened the garage door. He flipped on the light and saw that behind Lauren's car was a stack of plywood that could be used to cover the broken window.

"I'll admit I didn't jump on the fact that Lauren was missing as fast as I should have," Gary said. He leaned against the bumper of the car. "Hell, she was a grown woman and I figured if she didn't want to be found by her sister it was her choice. But when we found her body on the creek bed there was no question in my mind about what had happened, about how she had died." He rubbed his forehead as if he had the beginning of a headache. "Now, I'm going to have to rethink this whole thing, see what I missed and try to figure out what in the hell is going on around here."

For the first time in days Nick felt a bit of relief flood through him. He'd much rather have Gary on their side than thinking he and Lexie were a couple of conspiracy nuts.

"Nick, I probably wasn't the most sensitive man when your wife died and I've always been sorry about the way things wound up between us."

The apology shocked Nick. He knew how proud Gary was and the effort it cost him to say the words that had just fallen out of his mouth. "Water under the bridge," Nick replied gruffly. "Come on, let's get the window boarded up and then hopefully you can find out who in this town decided to pop off several rounds tonight," Nick said.

It took twenty minutes for the plywood to be put into place and then with Gary gone Nick and Lexie got to work cleaning up the broken glass.

"I hate to impose on you by staying at your house," she said, breaking the silence that had lingered between them since Gary had left.

"Nonsense, I have plenty of room and I wouldn't feel comfortable with you staying here alone after this," he replied. "Gary apologized to me out in the garage for the way he handled things when Danielle disappeared."

"That was big of him."

"It was," he agreed. "I definitely think he wants to find out who is responsible for this."

"I just feel like we're missing something." She leaned on the broom, her brow wrinkled in thought. "If Lauren's death was nothing more than an accident, then why would my presence here make somebody nervous enough to shoot up the house?"

"You're assigning a motive to the shooting that we don't know for sure is true," he replied. "It could have been bored teenagers out for a little rowdy fun who thought Lauren's house would be empty."

"You're right," she said and began to sweep using more force than necessary. "I'm just so frustrated."

"I know. Maybe by morning Gary will have some answers for us." Even as he said the words he didn't believe them and he had a feeling Lexie didn't believe them either.

It was almost nine o'clock when they finally left Lauren's place and headed to Nick's. Lexie had packed her things in a small suitcase that was loaded in the backseat along with Zeus, his food and water bowls and a huge bag of dog food.

Lexie had once again fallen silent and Nick didn't know what to say, what to do to bring her out of the shell she'd crawled into.

There was no question that he was worried about what had happened tonight. One of those bullets could have easily found either one of them. Who had shot the gun? What had they hoped to accomplish? Had it simply been some of the wild teenagers in town or had it been something darker…more dangerous? He shoved these thoughts aside as he pulled into his driveway.

When they got into his house the first thing they did was introduce Zeus to Taz. The little pooch raced around Zeus's legs until Zeus gave a warning growl. Taz hunkered down in front of the bigger dog, properly chastised.

Nick led Lexie to one of the guest rooms, wishing instead that she would warm his bed for the night, wanting a repeat of the lovemaking they'd shared before.

But he had a feeling that it had been emotional trauma and nothing more that had driven her into his arms on the night that Lauren's body had been found.

"Make yourself at home," he said as she placed her suitcase on the floor next to the bed. "The bathroom is across the hall, and if you need anything just let me know."

He suddenly realized he wanted her to need him. He wanted her to sleep with him because she wanted him more than any other man on the face of the earth. He wanted her driven by passion and desire and nothing more and it scared the hell out of him. He murmured a quick good-night, leaving her alone, and went back downstairs.

He checked that the doors were all locked and was surprised to find Taz curled up tight against Zeus's side in front of the fireplace. It looked like the two were going to be best buddies. Good. He wanted Zeus to have a home here. It was the least he could do in honor of the friend he'd lost and her sister.

When he climbed the stairs once again and got into his bedroom he sat on the edge of the bed and picked up the photo of Danielle from the nightstand. She had definitely been his one arrow. He'd loved her as deeply as a man could ever love a woman.

When they'd lost their baby he'd tried to be strong for her, thinking she needed his stoic strength, his broad shoulders. Then she'd accused him of not caring, of not grieving deeply and hard enough for the child they'd lost. He'd been unable to give her what she needed from him and there was a dark place in his heart that believed that was ultimately what had led to her suicide.

There was no question his feelings for Lexie were deepening with every moment he spent with her, but could he trust himself to try to be everything for a woman again? He'd already been there, done that and failed miserably.

He realized that as much as he desired Lexie, as much as he wanted only good things for her, he would never be willing to step up and try to have a long-term relationship with another woman.

LEXIE AWOKE WITH THE SUN streaming through the windows in Nick's guest room. She remained laying in bed, her mind flittering over the events of the night and dreading those to come.

Today the breeder was coming to take the rest of Lauren's dogs. Eventually she'd have to arrange for the sale of the house, and then there would be nothing left to mark the fact that Lauren had ever lived here in Widow Creek.

Lauren had come here with such high hopes, so excited to finally have the space, the perfect place and the opportunity to achieve her dreams. She'd been charmed by the small town, had raved about the people she was meeting each time she and Lexie had spoken on the phone.

Lauren had never mentioned anyone making her feel uncomfortable or scared in her new home. She'd only had positive things to say about Widow Creek.

Unexpected tears burned at Lexie's eyes, and she knew they weren't only tears for Lauren, but were also tears for herself. She knew she was offbeat, considered different by most people, but Lauren had always understood her. Lauren knew of her innate shyness, of her awkwardness when in a group of people. Lauren understood all that pieces that made up Lexie and now Lauren was gone forever.

She rolled over on her back and after wiping the tears away with the back of her hand, reached for her glasses on the nightstand. She put them on and as her thoughts once again turned to the night before a slow burn set off in her stomach.

There was something rotten in Widow Creek. She had no idea what it was or how deeply embedded the rot was, but there was no question in her mind that something was wrong here.

Had Lauren been murdered? The gunfire of the night before certainly made her believe that her presence here in town asking questions about her sister had made somebody very nervous. It was just too coincidental and Lexie didn't believe in that kind of coincidence.

Her thoughts turned to Nick. If she allowed herself, she realized she could be more than half-crazy about him. He was solid as a rock and sometimes when he looked at her she felt a shiver inside, a shiver of need, of want that she'd never felt before.

She would have liked nothing better than to crawl into his bed last night, but she'd also known it would be a mistake on her part.

With a sigh she rolled out of bed, grabbed clean clothes for the day and then darted across the hallway to the bathroom. She took a quick shower, used a squeeze of gel to spike her hair and then went in search of Nick.

She followed the scent of fresh-brewed coffee down the stairs to the kitchen, but instead of finding him there she found a note from him letting her know he was outside doing morning chores.

Both Taz and Zeus greeted her and after lots of scratching behind all ears, the two dogs stretched out on the kitchen floor side by side. Lexie looked at the big dog that Lauren had loved and once again her heart squeezed tight with pain.

Zeus would be happy here with Nick, she told herself. He already looked as if he'd made friends with the young pup next to him. Lauren would definitely be okay with this arrangement and Lexie found some peace at that thought.

She poured herself a cup of coffee and then, too restless to sit, she wandered back into the living room. This was a house meant for a family and as she thought about the baby and wife that Nick had lost her heart found a new ache, this time for him.

Lexie hadn't ever really had her heart broken. Oh, she'd thought at the time that Michael Andrews had broken it, but with time and distance away from his betrayal, she'd realized it hadn't been love that had driven her into his arms, only an intense loneliness.

He'd confirmed to her something that she'd always known deep in her heart—the fact that she was an outsider and would never have a real place that she belonged. Oh, she was good for a change of pace, a little walk on the weird side, but when it came to choosing somebody for a long-term relationship, Lexie would always be the one left behind for a more traditional woman.

She found herself climbing the stairs to the bedrooms and going past the room where she'd slept. She knew she was being nosy, but she wanted to see Nick's room.

The master suite was at the end of the hallway. She stood in the doorway and breathed in the scent of him that lingered in the air. She'd always felt safe and secure because she was an FBI agent and carried a gun, but there was no question that Nick made her feel safe and secure in a much different, more provocative kind of way.

She stared at the bed with its rumpled white sheets. The sheets would smell of him, perhaps still retain some of his body heat and there was nothing more she wanted at that moment than to climb in and close her eyes and wait for him to come back into the house and find her there.

Her gaze fell on the photograph on the nightstand and as she gazed at the attractive blonde woman her impulse to crawl into his bed died a sudden death.

Danielle.

His one arrow.

She was a pretty blonde with a bright smile. Her hair fell to her shoulders in soft waves and she was clad in a very proper dress in a mute shade of gold.

Nick had told her that Danielle had been a traditional kind of woman, one who enjoyed working as secretary for the mayor but also loved to bake cookies and work the social events the town offered.

Lexie was the antithesis of Danielle. She worked a job that put her in contact with criminals, wouldn't know how to bake a cookie that didn't come in a plastic tube and wanted to crawl out of her skin when surrounded by too many people.

The photo was a physical reminder to Lexie that Nick's heart had already been taken and that he didn't believe he had any part of his heart left to give to another.

Maybe he was helping her because he hadn't been able to help his wife. Maybe if he could be what Lexie needed him to be to get through this rough time, it would assuage some of the guilt she knew he felt over his wife's suicide. She wanted that for him. It would be nice if when she left this godforsaken place at least one of them would have complete peace.

She shoved these troubling thoughts to the back of her mind and hurried back down the stairs. She had just sat at the table when he came in the back door, bringing with him fresh autumn-scented air and a warm smile.

"I see you found the coffee," he said as he shrugged out of his jacket, exposing a revolver shoved into his waistband. He saw her look of surprise as he pulled out the revolver and laid it on the countertop. "Don't worry, I'm licensed to carry. After last night I decided I'd rather be armed and dangerous than unarmed and helpless."

"You're a smart man, Nick Walker," she replied dryly.

He poured himself a cup of coffee and joined her at the table. "Did you sleep okay?"

"Surprisingly well, given the events of the night," she replied. She took a sip of her coffee and tried not to notice how hot he looked in his jeans and tight, long-sleeved pullover. She didn't want to fall victim of his bedroom eyes and lose herself in a fantasy that would never come true.

"Want some breakfast?" he asked.

"No, coffee is fine for now," she replied.

"Want to talk about last night?"

"Until we have more information there isn't much to talk about," she countered. "Before we leave to meet the breeder I'm going to call my boss, Director Andrew Grimes, and let him know what's been happening here. I also need to tell him that I'm taking off some additional time until I'm satisfied with the investigation into Lauren's death."

"I'd like you to stay here with me until you decide to leave town. I definitely believe in the old adage that there's safety in numbers."

She didn't think it was a great idea, but Lexie also wasn't a fool. She recognized that she'd be safer if she was here with him rather than all alone at Lauren's place.

"If it's not too much of an imposition," she replied.

Again he flashed her that smile that warmed every cold inch that might linger in her body. "You're always worried about it being an imposition and you know it isn't. I like having you here. This house has been silent for far too long." He got up from the table. "And now I'm going to rustle me up some breakfast and then it will be time to head over to Lauren's to meet with the breeder."

He talked her into eating pancakes with him and once they cleaned up the mess it was time to head back to Lauren's place. The sight of the plywood where glass should have been in the front window sprang the terror of those few minutes of gunfire back into Lexie's brain.

It had been nothing short of a miracle that neither she nor Nick had been seriously hurt. What the shooting had done was lit a fire inside her to get to the bottom of things.

As they got out of the car the dogs in the pen at the side of the house greeted them with raucous barks of excitement. "Why don't I take care of feeding and watering the pups and you head inside and relax until Linetta gets here," Nick said.

Lexie nodded her agreement and they parted ways, Nick heading to the dog pen and Lexie stepping inside the house. With the front window boarded up the living room was dark. She flipped on a light and looked around and for a moment felt the aching absence of her sister.

She walked over to a bookcase where dozens of figurines of dogs were displayed. She found the German shepherd that Lauren had bought on the day she'd gotten Zeus.

Lexie picked it up and carried it into the kitchen where she wrapped it in a paper towel and then put it in her purse. It was just a cheap, silly piece of ceramic, but it had been Lauren's prized possession and it was the only thing Lexie wanted from this house.

She'd arrange for a local charity to take most of the items and then would list the place with a Realtor in the area. Hopefully it would sell quickly and Lexie wouldn't have to worry about being out of town with a vacant property to worry about.

She sat at the table and fought against a wave of sadness that threatened to overwhelm her. Funny in a sad kind of way that an entire lifetime could be packed up in boxes and given away to charity, she thought.

At least she didn't have to give up her memories of the sister she had loved. She only wished she and Lauren had taken time to make more memories with each other.

She had no time for sadness anymore. She needed to figure out why somebody had driven up the night before and fired bullets into the front window. She needed to know for certain if Lauren had really slipped and fallen to her death or if foul play had been involved.

Nick came into the kitchen. "All taken care of," he said as he went to the sink to wash his hands. Once he was finished he joined her at the table.

"I'm not weak," she said, and saw the momentary confusion that shadowed his eyes. She winced inwardly, aware that she should have prefaced her statement in some way. As usual her form of communication was awkward.

"I never thought you were," he replied.

She took off her glasses and leaned back in the chair. "I'm strong and decisive when I'm in front of a computer. I'm respected at work and I do a good job. I'm perfectly capable of taking care of myself and have never needed much from anyone."

"Why are you telling me this?"

She picked up her glasses and put them back on. "I just need you to understand that I'm not some weak, pathetic woman who needs a white knight to ride to her rescue."

He smiled at her. "Do I really look like a white knight? And keep in mind I do wear socks to bed every night."

"I just don't want to be your redemption."

He sat back in his chair and looked at her in confusion. "Lexie, what are you talking about?"

"Your wife. I'm talking about Danielle. I know you somehow blame yourself for her death." She saw his eyes darken and knew she'd touched a nerve. "I just don't want you to be here with me because you somehow feel that if you help me it will be your key to salvation."

"You obviously think too much. I'm here because I liked Lauren and more importantly because I like you. It's no more or less complicated than that."

At that moment the dogs outside began to bark, signaling the arrival of the breeder. Both Lexie and Nick got up to go outside to greet her.

Linetta Stone was built like a professional football tackle. Her short gray hair was tightly permed as if she had neither the time nor the inclination to deal with it. She was clad in a red flannel shirt and a pair of worn jeans and looked like a woman who didn't take crap from anyone.

As she climbed out of her truck her gaze was sharp and darted in all directions as if seeking any source of trouble that might come her way.

"Morning," she finally said.

Introductions were made and a hint of softness lit her eyes as she shook Lexie's hand. "Sorry to hear about your sister," she said. She rocked back on her heels and once again swept the area. "I have to admit, I was a little reluctant to drive in here, but I did a search on your sister and everything seemed to look legit."

"Why were you reluctant?" Nick asked.

"Widow Creek has a bit of a reputation. I thought it might be some sort of a scam. You know, where I get out here and somebody hits me over the head and takes any money I might have with me." She barked a laugh. "Although the joke would be on them, only thing I have in my wallet is my driver's license and an old picture of Blue, the first dog I ever owned."

"Why would you worry about somebody knocking you over the head?" Lexie asked.

"Drug fiends," Linetta said in a lowered voice. "This town is full of them."

Lexie looked at the older woman in surprise. "What kind of drugs?"

"Rumor has it Widow Creek is the place to come if you want meth. They make it and sell it out of their bathrooms, their sheds, their closets."

"Who does? Who makes it and sells it?" Lexie asked. Her mind boggled at this new piece of information.

Linetta's big shoulders moved up and down in a shrug. "I don't know who. It's just rumors. I heard it from my grandkid. He's sixteen and he's been told I'll take off a stripe of his hide if I ever hear he was in or around Widow Creek. Now, let's go take a look at those dogs."

As Lexie followed her to the pen her mind worked to digest what she'd just heard. Was it possible there was a major meth operation here in Widow Creek?

She knew enough about the making of methamphetamine to know that it could be manufactured in a bathroom or in a shed. The ingredients were easily obtained and it certainly didn't take a chemistry degree to put them all together. But here in Widow Creek? Wouldn't Nick have heard rumors about such a thing?

It didn't take long for Linetta to leave the pen and return to where Nick and Lexie awaited her. "They're terrific. They have friendly personalities and their overall health looks to be good. I'm sure I can find homes for all of them with no problems."

Minutes later Lexie watched as Nick and Linetta loaded the dogs into the cages waiting in the back of the breeder's truck. When the final dog was loaded and Linetta waved a goodbye and got into the truck, Lexie felt as if the last pieces of her sister were driving away from the house.

Nick looped an arm around her shoulder and she leaned against him and watched until the truck disappeared from sight. "You ready to head back to my place?" he asked.

She nodded and stepped away from him, her mind still working to process what she'd just learned from Linetta. It wasn't until she got into Nick's pickup that pieces began to fit together in her mind.

A rush of adrenaline filled her as Nick started the engine. "Did you know that Lauren was about to start training drug-sniffing dogs?"

"No, I didn't know that," he replied. He fastened his seat belt and then turned to look at her. "I seem to be asking you this all the time, but what are you thinking?"

"I'm thinking I might have just stumbled upon a motive for murder," she replied and watched his eyes widen in surprise.

Chapter Nine

"Think about it," Lexie said. "There's a big drug operation going on in the area and the people behind it discover that my sister is about to start training drug-sniffing dogs."

They were back in Nick's kitchen and seated at his table. Zeus was sleeping at Lexie's feet and Taz was chewing on a rawhide treat.

"And maybe the people in charge of the operation saw Lauren's newest venture as a threat to their business," Nick replied. "The last thing they'd want is a drug-sniffing dog running around town alerting on people and places. What this theory doesn't tell us is who is responsible…and it is just a theory," he reminded her.

She looked more alive than she had since the discovery of Lauren's body. Her green eyes snapped with life and a wild energy radiated from her, an energy that called to him, that made him want to sweep her into his arms and carry her up the stairs and into his bedroom.

Instead he tried to keep his mind focused on the conversation at hand. "But, it's the first real theory we've come up with," she replied. "And now what we need to do is prove or disprove it."

He frowned. "And how exactly do you intend to go about doing that?"

"I need to spend some more time in town, ask some subtle questions and see what kind of answers I get."

He gave her a wry grin. "You aren't exactly the subtle type, Lexie. I just don't want you to stir up somebody who decides to take potshots at us in the night again. The next time they might get lucky and actually hit one or both of us."

As much as he liked her, there was no doubt in his mind that, if what she believed was true, her style of asking questions would put a very large target on her back. Lexie was about as subtle as a pit bull.

Her cheeks grew pink. "You're right. But if I just hang out in town I should at least be able to tell if somebody is using or not. People using meth aren't able to fly under the radar very well."

"Euphoria, paranoia, acne, sores, weight loss, a lack of personal hygiene." He smiled as she looked at him in surprise. "Don't worry, I learned everything I know about it from a documentary on television. I like documentaries—it's one of those nerdy things about me. You know, we could ask Gary what kind of a problem drug use is in the town."

She shook her head. "I'd rather keep this to ourselves for the time being."

"You still don't trust Gary?" he asked.

Her beautiful green eyes held his in a gaze he felt

pierce clear through to his heart. "The only person I have left in the world that I trust without question right now is you, Nick."

In that moment Nick felt as if he'd been given a precious gift. He had a feeling Lexie wasn't a woman who trusted easily, and the fact that she trusted him made him want to jump up and grab the moon for her if that's what she needed.

"So, what's the game plan, Agent Forbes?" he asked.

She gave him a tight smile. "I'm thinking we go to the café for dinner tonight and then maybe find out if we can figure out where the young people hang out when the sun goes down. If anyone knows if there are drugs available here in Widow Creek it's probably going to be the teenagers."

Nick leaned back in his chair, a slow burn of anxiety beginning in his gut. "If what you think is true, then these people are very dangerous. They've killed Lauren and could have killed both of us."

She narrowed her eyes slightly. "So, does that mean you want out? Nick, I'd certainly understand if you do. This isn't your battle to fight."

"Of course it's my battle. This is my town." It was the easy answer, but the truth of the matter was it had become his battle the moment his mouth had taken hers on the night they'd made love. It had become his battle when he'd held her in his arms as she'd cried over her sister's death.

"I think maybe I'll take a little nap, if you don't

mind," she said as she pushed back from the table. "It's been kind of a stressful morning."

"Go on, get some rest," he replied. "We'll talk about everything else later."

As she disappeared from the kitchen Nick remained seated in his chair. He realized that saying goodbye to Lauren's dogs had been more difficult for her than she'd let on.

It had been the same for him when he'd donated Danielle's clothing and shoes to a local charity. It had been almost six months after her death and he'd thought he was ready, but folding the clothes and placing them in boxes, picking up the shoes and remembering when she'd worn them last had slammed his grief back into him in a way he hadn't expected.

His mind shifted back to his conversation with Lexie. Drugs in Widow Creek? Nick didn't want to believe it, but during the past year he hadn't spent a lot of time in town. He'd isolated himself too much, he realized. He'd pulled his grief around him and wallowed in it and it was past time he changed that.

It was time he find out what was going on in his hometown, time he stop isolating himself and truly integrate himself back into life in Widow Creek.

Every town probably had a drug problem of sorts, but Nick knew from the documentary he'd watched that meth had become the scourge of small-town America. Meth labs were dangerous not only because of the drug they produced, but also because of the chemicals needed to make that drug.

He got up from the table and went up the stairs. He passed the guest room where Lexie had gone. The door was closed and he hoped she was resting peacefully. Between the funeral yesterday and the shooting and then giving the dogs away today, she had to be emotionally exhausted.

He went on into his bedroom and instantly saw the photo of Danielle on his nightstand. As always his heart squeezed at the sight of her, but this time his grief wasn't the cutting, breath-stealing force it had always been. It was simply the ache of loss that was natural after saying goodbye to a loved one.

Was his desire to help Lexie his need to somehow find some sort of redemption as she'd suggested? Did he believe that in being there for Lexie he could mitigate some of the guilt he felt about Danielle?

He didn't believe it. The minute he'd seen Lexie she had touched him in a way he hadn't been touched in a very long time. That night that he'd met her in Lauren's house it should have been easy for him to walk away from her, but he'd been unable to do so.

Her awkwardness drew him, her quirky little smile warmed him and there were moments now when he couldn't imagine what his life would be like when she was gone.

But he knew he couldn't think that way. Lexie didn't belong here. She had her life, her work in Kansas City. Once she had the answers she needed to find peace, she would be gone. And besides, he had already made the decision that he was destined to live here alone.

Zeus came running into the room, chased by the rascal Taz. Both dogs stopped in their tracks at the sight of him, as if they were two kids caught with their hands in the cookie jar. Deciding they both could use a run outside, he placed the picture of Danielle in the nightstand drawer and then left the bedroom and headed downstairs, the dogs close at his heels.

He sat on the deck and watched the two dogs frolic in the fallen leaves and went over things in his mind. He didn't know what to believe about Lauren's death and the drug angle. All he knew was that he was in this until the end…even though he knew that in the end he would have to tell Lexie goodbye.

It was almost six o'clock when Nick and Lexie left the house to go into town for dinner. She'd awakened an hour earlier and had showered and changed, but had been unusually quiet since leaving the bedroom.

"You should be starving," he said once they were in the truck and headed into Widow Creek. "You slept through lunch and you didn't do much more than pick at your breakfast."

"I wasn't sleeping the whole time. I called my boss and checked in with him and then called a friend of mine, a fellow agent, Amberly Nightsong, and yes, I am a little bit hungry, but I'd rather get information than food."

"Let's hope we get both," Nick replied.

They fell silent once again and not for the first time Nick wished he could get inside her head, see what she was thinking, know exactly what she was feeling.

When had it happened? When in the course of the five days since he'd met her had her thoughts become so important to him? When had his need to know everything about her become so intense?

She remained quiet through their meal at the Cowboy Corral, eating very little and instead keeping her attention focused on the other diners.

Nick saw nobody that he thought might be under the influence of drugs. He also saw none of the teenagers of the town inside the restaurant.

"You might try eating some of that food instead of moving it around on your plate," he said.

She looked down at the chicken-fried steak dinner she'd ordered and then up at him. "You're food obsessed."

He smiled. "And you don't eat enough to keep a bird alive."

"That's not true. I can eat my weight in hot wings."

He laughed. "I'd like to see that."

"I should probably warn you, it usually involves a six-pack of beer at the same time." Her smile fell and once again her gaze darted around the room.

"You know, we might have more luck tomorrow night," he said as they lingered over coffee. "It's Thursday night and school is in session. It's doubtful any of the teens would be out late tonight doing illegal activities. We'd probably have better luck tomorrow or Saturday night."

"That makes sense," she agreed reluctantly. She picked up her cup and took a sip. "Maybe Linetta

Stone's rumors were just that, silly rumors with no fact." Her voice held a weariness of spirit that reached inside him and squeezed his heart.

"Lexie, just because we didn't find what we were looking for in a two-hour meal on a Thursday night doesn't mean that what we're looking for isn't here."

"You're right," she replied and sat up straighter in her chair. "I'm just impatient. Lauren used to tell me all the time that unlike my computer where things happen with the click of the mouse, real life requires more patience."

"We'll come back tomorrow night," he promised. "And the night after that and the night after that. We'll do this however long it takes for you to get some peace of mind. And after we eat dinner if we don't see anybody who might give us some answers we'll drive around town and find out where the kids all hang out."

"Where did you hang out when you were a teenager?" she asked when they were in his truck and headed back to his house.

"When I was young there was a bowling alley and a movie theater and most weekends that's where all the kids gathered. But both of those businesses closed down years ago. What about you? Where did you hang out?" he asked, hoping to steer the conversation away from drugs and Lauren's death at least for a few minutes.

"I didn't hang out a lot when I was a teenager. Occasionally Lauren would twist my arm and I'd reluctantly go with her and some of her friends to a pizza place where a lot of the kids hung out. As I'm sure you've noticed, I'm not at my best in a crowd, so I didn't go often. I spent a lot of time with my dad," she replied.

"What was he like?" He cast her a quick glance and saw the softening of her features as she thought of her father.

"He was the best," she replied. "He took us fishing and painted our fingernails. He baked cookies for school functions and taught us how to play basketball. He was both mom and dad to us and did a good job at being both. He knew I struggled with my shyness, with my awkwardness, but he always made me feel special. When he died I knew I'd lost my best champion."

"There hasn't been any other important man in your life?"

She gazed out the side window. "Only Michael, and I already told you about him." She turned back to look at him. "I thought he might be my one real Cupid's arrow, but he was just a silly misfire."

She sat up straighter in the seat as he pulled into his drive. "I just wish I knew whether we were onto something here or if we're just spinning our wheels."

"Hopefully we'll know by the end of the weekend," he replied. "If we take each troubling incident separately they don't add up to much. You saw somebody in the back of Lauren's place lurking in the middle of the night right before her body was found. You believe that Lauren's body was placed on the creek bed long after she was killed. Somebody shot up Lauren's place. When you add them altogether and throw in a drug angle, it's all more than troubling. It feels criminal."

"So, you don't think I'm crazy?" she asked.

"Definitely not," he replied as he pulled up in front of his house.

As they walked inside Taz and Zeus greeted them with happy barks. Nick tried not to think about how right it felt for Lexie to be by his side, tried not to notice how the house filled with her very presence.

It was going to be hard for him when she went back to Kansas City. The house would once again radiate with the emptiness that had become all too familiar over the last year of his life. Dogs were great companions, but they didn't quite take the place of human beings.

"You want some more coffee?" he asked as they went into the kitchen. "I could make a pot."

"No thanks. I drank enough coffee for one day."

"How about a glass of wine?"

She hesitated a moment and then nodded. "Sure, that would be great. White if you have it."

"I do," he replied. "Why don't you make yourself comfortable in the living room and I'll bring it to you."

"Sounds like a plan." She left the kitchen with the dogs trailing at her heels.

Nick poured them each a glass of wine and then carried it into the living room where she was seated on the sofa. He handed her a glass and then sank down next to her.

Throughout the evening he'd been acutely aware of her on a physical level. He'd found the familiar scent of her intoxicating and couldn't help but notice the way her green sweater hugged her breasts.

It had been difficult for him to keep his mind on the reason they had been in the café, difficult to keep his mind away from the night they'd made love.

He wanted her again. He wanted to taste her lips, feel the warmth of her naked in his arms. It was more than a simple want, it was a growing need that was getting more and more difficult to ignore.

"Tell me about the fall festival," she said. She took off her glasses and set them on the coffee table and then leaned back against the sofa cushion. "You mentioned it was one of the things that brought the whole town together."

"It's always the first week in November. The stores close down for the day and Main Street becomes a playground for everyone. The mayor's office provides a bean feast with pots of beans and corn bread. There are pie-eating contests and carnival rides and something to bring a smile to everyone's faces."

"Sounds wonderful," she replied.

"It's definitely small town at its best." He stared down into his wine glass, recognizing that in all probability when the fall festival in less than a month occurred Lexie would be long gone. "Maybe you could come back here for the festival."

"Maybe," she agreed, but he had a feeling they both knew that it was doubtful that once she left she'd ever return to Widow Creek, except occasionally to visit her sister's grave.

"More wine?" he asked as he noticed her glass was empty.

"Maybe just a little."

He got up from the sofa and returned to the kitchen for the bottle and used the opportunity to attempt to tamp down the desire that seemed to be building to mammoth proportions as the night continued.

He returned to the living room and any efforts he thought he'd made to get control of his hormones vanished. He felt like a nervous teenager out with the prettiest cheerleader, desperate to make a move on her, but afraid at the same time.

He poured her wine and set the bottle on the table, then leaned back and smiled at her. "You look pretty tonight. You should wear green more often."

She smiled self-consciously and reached for her glasses. "Thanks. You look very nice yourself." She put her glasses back on, took a sip of her wine and then ran her tongue over her top lip.

The desire that had been simmering inside him all night long exploded into a flame. "Lexie." Her name escaped his lips of its own volition. He set his glass on the coffee table and then reached out and removed hers from her hand and placed it next to his.

Her eyes widened behind her glasses, as if she knew his intent. He wrapped his hand around the back of her neck and gently pulled her toward him.

Chapter Ten

His mouth was hot against hers and tasted of wine and a heady intoxication flooded through her veins. He was an assault on every one of her senses. The familiar scent of him filled her head, the heat of his mouth warmed her to her toes and when he reached to embrace her she allowed him to pull her closer…closer still.

She wanted him like she needed her next breath, desperately, viscerally. And ultimately it was the depth of her want of him that forced her away from him and to her feet.

"Nick, we can't do this anymore." Her own breathlessness surprised her. "I don't want you to kiss me anymore." Her gaze fled to the furthest corner of the room.

"I'm sorry," he replied. "I…I guess I got my signals crossed."

Her cheeks flushed pink. "No, I've probably been giving off mixed signals to you." She pulled off her glasses and rubbed her eyes as unexpected tears stung. "I want you, Nick, but I just don't think it's a good idea for us to be intimate again. I'll be leaving here as soon as I get some answers and I've never been good with casual sex." *Or goodbyes*, she thought.

"It didn't seem casual to me," he replied, his eyes dark and enigmatic.

"But we both know that's what it was," she replied. She hesitated a beat, giving him an opportunity to make her believe otherwise. When he didn't say anything she released a deep sigh.

"I think I'll just call it a night," she said and although she put her glasses back on her eyes didn't quite meet his. "I'll just see you in the morning."

She felt as if this had been a defining moment, that something had happened that had forever changed things between them.

What had changed was that the little bit of hope Lexie hadn't even realized she'd entertained in her heart about Nick had just died. It had been the hope that his heart might be capable of realizing love for a second time in his life, the hope that he might be falling in love with her.

She had to tell him goodbye.

Lexie sat on the edge of the bed in the guest bedroom and knew she had to get away from Nick. She was in love with him. It had crept upon her insidiously, without warning. It had been fed not only by his warm smile and sense of humor, but also by his seemingly easy acceptance of all that she was as a woman—and of all that she wasn't.

She had to get out before things went any deeper.

Already it was going to pierce her very core to have to tell him goodbye.

With this thought in mind she grabbed her cell phone out of her purse and made a call. When she hung up after having a long conversation with her friend and coworker Amberly Nightsong, she waited for the sense of relief to flood through her. But there was no relief, only sadness as she realized it was time for her to make some changes.

It was just her luck, to fall in love with a man who was emotionally unavailable. First Michael the jerk, and then Nick, a man who had known a love so great it was apparently enough to last him a lifetime despite the fact that the woman he loved was dead.

She couldn't even be mad at Nick. He'd warned her from the very beginning that he'd had his one arrow shot in the heart and wasn't looking for another. It was her own fault for being foolish enough to fall in love with him.

She changed into her nightgown and got into bed, her heart as heavy as a stone. In the very depths of her soul she'd always worried that she'd been destined to be alone, to never really know the wonder of a man's love. She squeezed her eyes tightly closed as tears once again burned.

There had been moments when she'd thought she'd felt love from Nick, when his eyes had glowed with emotion, when his kiss had tasted of not just desire, but of something deeper, something more profound. She'd been a fool.

Time and distance, that what's she needed. She wasn't ready to leave Widow Creek, but it was time she left Nick Walker and gave herself time to heal.

The next morning she carried her suitcase down to the kitchen where she found Nick seated at the table eating a muffin and drinking a cup of coffee. As usual both dogs were at his feet, looking perfectly content to relax in the sunshine that drifted in through the window.

"Good morning," he said and looked pointedly at her suitcase. "Going somewhere?"

"I'm checking into the local motel this morning," she said.

He looked at her in surprise and got out of his chair. "Lexie, if this is about what happened last night—"

"It is…and it isn't," she interrupted him. "Nick, you've given me enough of your time and energy. I appreciate everything you've done for me and all the support you've given me, but this really isn't your battle and it's time I move on."

"Lexie, I don't want you to be alone. I don't think it's safe," he protested.

"I won't be alone," she assured him. "An FBI friend of mine is meeting me at the motel this afternoon. She's going to stay with me for a couple of days. It's better this way, Nick. Better for both of us."

He looked as if he wanted to protest but after a moment he simply nodded. "I guess there's nothing I can say to change your mind." She shook her head and he continued, "Then just know that I'm here for you if you need me."

Although this was exactly what she wanted to hear from him, she couldn't help the small flutter of disappointment that he hadn't tried to change her mind, hadn't insisted that she stay here with him.

"Want to stick around for some breakfast?" he asked.

Again she shook her head. "No, thanks. I'm just going to head on out and get settled in at the motel."

He walked toward her and she steeled herself for his nearness, afraid that somehow she might fall into the gray depths of his eyes and lose herself forever.

He placed his palms on either side of her face and stared deep into her eyes. "Call me, Lexie. Let me know what's going on. Let me know that you're okay. It's important to me, okay?"

His touch made her ache and she fought against the need to lean into him, to feel his arms embrace her one last time. She stepped back and he dropped his hands to his sides. "I will," she agreed. "And you'll take good care of Zeus?"

"Of course, he's part of my family now."

She thought about how happy she would be to be part of his family and this propelled her out of the kitchen and toward the front door. She was aware of Nick following right behind her, but when she reached the door she didn't stop. She didn't want any long goodbyes. She just wanted to get gone, away from his concerned eyes, away from the scent of him that smelled so much like home.

She didn't stop walking until she reached her car. She opened the door, threw her suitcase in the backseat and only then did she turn to look at him. "Thanks again, Nick."

"Keep in touch, Lexie."

"I will." She slid into the seat, closed her door and started the engine. She refused to look in her rearview mirror as she pulled away. She was afraid that one more glimpse of him might make her cry, and that would be foolish.

She hadn't even cried when Michael had left her and they had dated off and on for months. It was crazy that in six days Nick had managed to get so deep into her heart.

But there was no happy ending and she knew the best thing she could do was cast him out of her thoughts and hope that eventually her heart would forget him.

She checked into the Stop and Sleep Motel, the only such establishment of its kind in the small town. The room held two double beds covered in gold spreads and the gold shag rug on the floor was obviously the original. She might have found it depressing, but she knew when Amberly arrived the decor couldn't matter.

She sat on the bed and thought of the gorgeous Native American woman who would be arriving in the next couple of hours. Amberly worked as a profiler. She was also the single mother of a four-year-old named Max and she and her ex-husband shared custody of the little boy.

Lexie and Amberly had struck up a friendship a little over a year ago. She not only told wonderful stories from her Cherokee grandmother, but she understood all of Lexie's quirks and seemed to accept them.

Amberly arrived just after noon. Her butt-length black hair was pulled back in a careless chignon and eyes as dark as tar pits snapped with energy as she carried in her suitcase.

"Nothing like a little road trip to get the juices flowing," she said as she gave Lexie a hug. She stepped back from her and frowned. "You look like you've been beaten up with a tired stick."

Lexie smiled. "It's good to see you, too."

"I'm so sorry about Lauren."

Lexie's heart constricted in her chest as she nodded. "Sit down and let me tell you about everything that's happened."

It took nearly two hours for Lexie to share with Amberly everything that had happened since she'd arrived in Widow Creek. "But I really didn't invite you here to get involved in my investigation. I just didn't want to stay here in the motel by myself and I knew I'd enjoy your company for a couple of days."

"I'm interested in your theory of what's going on here, but I'm equally interested in this Nick Walker," Amberly said when Lexie was finished.

"Why?" Lexie asked in surprise.

"Because he obviously means something to you. It's evident every time you say his name. You get a soft, gooey look in your eyes."

Lexie felt her face fill with heat. "I do not," she exclaimed and then released a sigh. "In any case it doesn't matter. He's a widower still very much tied to his dead wife." As she told Amberly about Danielle's suicide she tried not to allow her emotions full rein.

"My grandmother would say that the moon god has captured his heart and refuses to let it go to find love again."

"Is that an old Cherokee legend?" Lexie asked.

Amberly flashed a bright smile. "No, that's a Granny Nightsong legend. She was an expert at making things up to fit any circumstance."

Lexie grinned at her. "I would have loved your granny. How are things at work?" Lexie asked in an attempt to keep the conversation away from Nick.

"Slow, which is good."

"And how's Max?"

Again the beautiful smile swept over Amberly's features. "He's the most amazing kid on the face of the earth."

"And what about men? Are you seeing anyone?"

Amberly shook her head. "Right now I have a good relationship with John, I have Max and I have my work and that's all I need. Besides, I've pretty much decided no dating until Max is older."

"Have you ever thought about you and John getting back together?" Lexie asked. She knew John and Amberly had been married for three years and had divorced when Max was two, but they seemed to share a special bond that hadn't been broken by the divorce.

"John and I were meant to be best friends, not lovers," she replied.

The two women stayed in the motel room catching up with each other until dinnertime, then headed for the café for their evening meal and to check out the locals.

"I give this place another two or three years and it will be a ghost town," Amberly observed as Lexie drove down Main Street. "It looks like it is already dead and nobody has mentioned it to the people who have remained."

"Just another victim of the bad economy," Lexie said as she pulled into a parking place in front of the café.

"Like so many other small towns," Amberly replied. "It's sad, isn't it? Mayberry towns are dying every day and soon there won't be any left."

As they walked into the busy café Lexie couldn't help but remember the meals she'd eaten here with Nick and she mentally cursed herself for allowing him to get too close, for allowing herself to fall so hard for a man so wrong for her.

She saw the table of teenagers as soon as they were seated in a nearby booth. There were four of them, two boys and two girls, and as the waitress took their orders it was evident by the expression on her face that she found them both rude and obnoxious.

What Lexie couldn't discern from her distance from the four is if it was just normal teenage rebelliousness or something else.

"You know, it's possible the people using in this town aren't teenagers at all. Meth use crosses age, economic and social boundaries," Amberly said softly. "It's the scourge of the earth as far as I'm concerned."

"I'm just hoping we find somebody who is using and can get them to answer some questions," Lexie replied.

Amberly laughed. "You're going to ask them who their source is and they're just going to answer you? That's a little naive, Lexie."

"I didn't say I thought they would answer me, but it doesn't hurt to ask. When I do identify somebody I think is using then I intend to watch them day and night. Eventually they'll take me to their source," Lexie explained.

Amberly leaned forward, her eyes coals of intensity. "Lexie, you're sure what you're doing here? Are you sure you aren't seeing boogeymen in an effort to explain a senseless tragedy?"

"It wasn't imaginary boogeymen who shot up Lauren's place," Lexie replied.

"True, but didn't the chief of police mention that there had been other instances of kids shooting at houses and barns?"

"Yes, but that doesn't explain that Lauren's body wasn't on that rocky shore when I first arrived here and checked." She released a sigh of frustration. "Amberly, have you ever had a gut instinct that you can't dismiss? That's what I feel…that something isn't right here and Lauren got into somebody's way. The drug angle is the only thing that halfway makes sense."

At that moment the waitress arrived to take their orders. When the meal arrived Lexie picked at the food and kept her focus on the four teenagers. One of the males, dark-haired and slightly unkempt, looked spun, as if he'd been up for days. He scratched his belly and picked at his face and a rush of adrenaline filled Lexie as the four got up and headed to the cashier.

"I've got a live one. You wait here and I'll be right back," she said to Amberly. Before her friend could protest, Lexie slid out of the booth and followed the teens outside.

"Hey," she called after them. The four of them turned as a unit.

"Hey yourself," the dark-haired boy said and then snickered as if he'd been remarkably clever. Up close Lexie could see the acnelike sores that covered his jaw and hovered around his mouth. *Definitely a meth-head,* she thought.

"Cool hair," one of the girls said with a friendly smile.

"Thanks. By the way, I'm Lexie Forbes. I'm new here in Widow Creek."

"And my name is Jimmy Carter," meth-head replied.

The girl with him poked him with her elbow. "Don't be stupid. He's Jimmy all right, but he's not Jimmy Carter, he's Jimmy Morano." The girl went on to introduce the others and then frowned at Lexie. "Was there something you wanted?"

"I was just wondering what people did for fun around here," Lexie replied. "Any private clubs where you can find something a little more fun than booze?"

Instantly she knew she'd pushed too fast, too hard. Jimmy's eyes narrowed. "What are you, some kind of a narc?"

Lexie forced a silly grin. "Duh, do I look like a narc?" she countered. She allowed the grin to fall. "Look, my sister just died and I'm stuck in this small town until I can sell her house. I can party like a rock star in Kansas City, but I need something now to make me feel better."

"Then go see your doctor," Jimmy replied. He turned on his heels. "Come on, let's get out of here."

As he walked away with two of the others, the girl who had been with him looked at Lexie, her eyes dark and slightly frightened. "You'd be better off going back to Kansas City to party. You don't want to ask too many questions here in Widow Creek."

Before Lexie could say anything else, the girl whirled around and ran after her friends. As Lexie watched the four head down the sidewalk she knew with a certainty that Jimmy Morano, aka Jimmy Carter, and his girlfriend were her key to solving the mystery of Lauren's death.

All she had to figure out was how to make them cooperate with her before the people in charge got wind that she was onto them and tried to shut her up permanently.

NICK HAD THOUGHT the silence of the house after Danielle had moved out was bad, but the deafening silence that Lexie had left behind was a hundred times worse.

All day Saturday Nick felt her absence in a way he hadn't expected. It rang in the hallways of his house, seeped through the living room and into the kitchen like a gray fog.

He caught up on chores, played with the dogs and wondered what Lexie was doing, if she were eating properly. He worried about that. In his short experience with her, she didn't eat when she needed to. She needed somebody watching over her, making sure she was getting proper nutrition.

Not your job, he reminded himself again and again. She didn't need him to take care of her, she was perfectly capable of taking care of herself.

Still, by dinnertime that night he broke down and called her cell phone, which resulted in a brief, awkward conversation with her assuring him she was just fine.

By five on Sunday night he was sick of his own company and decided to head into town for dinner. The truth of the matter was the café was the only place in town to eat and he was hoping to see Lexie and her friend there.

Disappointment fluttered through him as he walked in and looked around. There was no sign of Lexie, but he told himself it was still relatively early for dinner. He took a stool at the counter and smiled at Marge.

"What's up?" he asked.

"My blood pressure," she replied with a wry grin. "What's up with you? I see you've lost your little side-kick. Did she go back where she came from?"

"No, she's still here in town. She's staying with a friend. So, what's the special of the day?"

Nick had just finished his burger and fries when

they walked in and his heart leapt at the sight of her. Lexie was clad in her usual pair of jeans and wore a purple, sequined long-sleeved T-shirt that hugged her curves like a lover. She was with a tall, attractive Native American woman.

In that first initial glimpse of him a smile of what appeared to be unadulterated joy burst over her features, a smile that quickly tempered into something less.

They nodded to each other and then she and her friend walked toward the back where a booth had become available. It wasn't enough. He realized just seeing her wasn't enough to fill him up.

He waited until they'd given their order to the waitress and then he got up off his stool and walked to their booth. "Hi, Nick. This is my friend, Amberly Nightsong," Lexie said.

"Amberly, nice to meet you," he replied.

"Nick, why don't you join us," Amberly said with a friendly smile.

"I've already eaten, but maybe I could sit for a cup of coffee," he agreed. He slid in next to Lexie, breathed in her familiar scent and tried not to notice how she tensed with his nearness.

"Lexie has told me all about you, Nick," Amberly said.

"And you're still willing to let me sit here with you," he said jokingly.

"I've told her what a support you've been to me," Lexie replied.

"And I appreciate you taking care of my friend," Amberly said.

"It's been my pleasure." In fact, it had been more than his pleasure. Lexie had brought him back to life, filled him with an excitement that had been missing for too long. "Have you managed to find out anything in the last two days?" he asked in a lowered voice.

He tried to stay focused on what Lexie told him about Jimmy Morano instead of dwelling on how much he wanted to take her back to his house, how much he'd like to wake up in the morning with her back under his roof.

"I know the Morano family. George works at the post office and his wife, Sarah, works at the grocery store. Jimmy is their only child. They'd be appalled if he's gotten himself hooked up in some drug scheme."

"Amberly and I have been following him since Friday night, but so far he hasn't led us anywhere interesting," Lexie said. "But if he's like any meth-head, it won't be long and he'll be contacting his source for a score. When he does I'll have another piece of the puzzle."

"Are you sure it isn't time to take your suspicions to Gary?" he asked.

"Gary?" Amberly looked at Lexie. "Who's Gary?"

"Chief of Police Gary Wendall. And, no, I'm not ready to take this to him," Lexie replied. "I'm not convinced he's completely innocent in whatever is going on in this town."

"I just don't want to see you doing all this alone," Nick said.

"I'm not alone. I have Amberly with me," she replied.

Silence reigned and in that silence Nick realized he was making Lexie uncomfortable. At that moment the waitress arrived with their orders and Nick slid out of the booth. "I'll just leave you two alone to enjoy your meal."

"I thought you were going to have coffee," Amberly protested.

"Nah, I'd better be on my way." He looked at Lexie and was shocked by the wave of sadness that suddenly hit him.

Something had broken between them. When he'd kissed her that last time he could have sworn she'd answered the kiss with a sweet longing. He'd been certain that she wanted him as badly as he wanted her. But she had been right to halt the kiss, to stop whatever might follow.

He stepped out of the café and into the evening autumn air, and a deep depression settled over his shoulders as he headed toward his truck.

He told himself it was for the best, that he had nothing to offer her except a temporary passion. He knew they had been getting in too deep with each other and it was probably a good thing she'd not only called a halt to another night of passion, but also had moved out of his house.

He got into his truck and leaned his head back before starting the engine. She'd blown into Widow Creek, pink hair, sparkly shirts and all, and had turned his life upside down.

Her escape from his last kiss had felt oddly like a goodbye. What shocked him more than anything was how much he didn't want to tell her goodbye.

Chapter Eleven

"He's hot," Amberly said.

The two women were back in the motel room and in their beds. Lexie didn't pretend not to know exactly who her friend was talking about. "Yes, he is, but that doesn't matter. He's unavailable."

"Such a shame. Still, he looked at you like he wanted to gobble you up for dessert."

"I didn't say he was sexually unavailable," Lexie said dryly. "He's just emotionally unable to move forward in another relationship."

Her heart squeezed tight in her chest. The last person she wanted to talk about at the moment was Nick. The sight of him in the café had been almost more than she'd been able to bear. And when he'd slid in next to her in the booth she'd wanted nothing more than to melt against him in utter surrender.

"I can't believe we're no closer to finding out who Jimmy's source for drugs is," Lexie said in an attempt to change the subject. She rolled over on her side in her bed and looked at Amberly in the bed next to her.

"Maybe Jimmy wasn't tweaking when we saw him

Friday night. Maybe he's just a hyper kid with bad skin who isn't fond of good hygiene."

"Maybe, but he looked like he was tweaking to me," Lexie replied.

"Lexie, we followed that kid through the weekend and he didn't do anything more exciting than pick his nose when he thought nobody was looking."

It was true. They'd shadowed Jimmy Morano as he'd left his house on Saturday morning, raked leaves at a neighbor's house for two hours and then hung out with friends in front of an empty store lot. Today had been much the same with them tailing Jimmy as he did nothing out of the ordinary for a teenager. He'd gone to church with his parents then had played a game of tag football with a bunch of other kids in an empty lot and finally had returned home.

Lexie released a deep sigh. To make matters worse, a few minutes earlier Amberly had received a call and needed to return to Kansas City the next day.

Thoughts of Nick once again filled Lexie's mind, just as they had every other minute since she'd left his house.

He haunted her in ways she'd never been haunted before, invading her dreams when she slept and filling her head with memories of their time together.

Driven by grief and need she'd slept with him and now she found herself wishing she'd made love to him one last time with only her love for him driving her into his arms.

Besides seeing him in the café that evening he'd

called her the day before, resulting in a brief conversation that had made her feel bereft when they'd hung up. The mere sound of his voice had caused her heart to ache.

"So, what are you going to do about Nick?" Amberly asked, as if she'd been able to read Lexie's thoughts.

Lexie rolled over on her back and stared up at the ceiling. "Nothing. There's nothing to do. He has no desire to be with another woman and, besides, I wouldn't be right for him anyway."

"And why is that?"

Once again Lexie turned to face her friend. "Aside from the fact that he lives and works here and I live and work in Kansas City, Nick is a small-town, traditional kind of man. He'd never really consider a long-term relationship with an offbeat woman like me."

"Lexie, you're the only person who thinks you're offbeat. That's the identity you gave yourself to be different than Lauren. The truth is you're no more offbeat than any other person on this planet."

"You aren't offbeat," Lexie protested.

"The hell I'm not," Amberly exclaimed. "I'll only sleep on the left side of the bed. I make Max wear a necklace and I worry that if he ever loses it or it comes off his neck something bad will happen. I only like mac and cheese if it's burnt and I'm addicted to red licorice. We all have little quirks that others find a little strange."

"But Michael told me I was too weird for him when he broke up with me," Lexie reminded her.

"Lexie, Michael was a dirtbag. He would have tried

to convince you that you were an alien if it served his own selfish needs."

A giggle escaped Lexie and for the next hour the two talked about every dreadful date they'd ever been on. It was only when Amberly fell asleep that Lexie's thoughts once again went to Nick and tears burned behind her eyelids.

Maybe she should just leave Widow Creek tomorrow when Amberly left. Maybe she should just accept Lauren's death as an accident and get back to her life in Kansas City.

It wasn't her job to clean up any problems that might exist in Widow Creek. It wasn't her duty to try to do Gary's job. She could go to him with all her suspicions, lay it out on the table and then leave town.

But the next morning she was more determined than ever to get to the bottom of the case. "Call me if you need anything," Amberly said as she got into her car to leave. "And don't try to be a hero. If you need backup, ask for it."

Lexie watched as Amberly's car disappeared down the highway and then she went back into her motel room. Jimmy would be at school until three that afternoon so there was really nothing she could do in the meantime. She still believed he was her ticket to finding out who was the source for the drugs.

She tried not to think about the fact that she was truly on her own now in a town where she didn't know who to trust. At three o'clock she was parked down the street from Jimmy's house, waiting for the teen to get home from school.

Maybe today would be the day the kid would lead her someplace where she could get a handle on who might be selling drugs in Widow Creek. Once she had that person in her sights she could work up the chain of command to find the person behind it all, the person she believed was ultimately responsible for Lauren's death.

Unless you're making this all up, a little voice whispered in the back of her brain. As long as she was thinking about drug connections and nefarious characters, she wasn't thinking about Lauren and she wasn't thinking about Nick.

It could be argued that there was a logical explanation for everything that had happened. Lauren really could have slipped and fallen to her death on the rocks by the creek and Lexie simply hadn't seen her body on the night she'd searched.

The shooting could be nothing more than stupid teenagers performing a daring drive-by at the house of a dead woman and that Linetta Stone could have passed on nothing more than malicious gossip.

She sat up straighter in her seat as the high school bus lumbered into view. And maybe Jimmy Morano really was just a teenage kid with bad hygiene and acne.

Maybe her mind had subconsciously tied all these things together in a big bow of desperation so that she'd have something to focus on other than the grief that was never far from the surface. Not to mention the loneliness that she knew awaited her when she finally went back home.

She watched as Jimmy got off the bus with what looked like a younger girl. The two didn't talk and Jimmy made a direct beeline to his house while the girl walked in the opposite direction.

Lexie settled back in her seat, knowing it might be hours before he left his house again…hours when she'd have nothing to do but think.

And as always, when she had a minute to herself, she thought of Nick. She'd spent most of the day trying to convince herself that she didn't really love him, that her feelings for him had gotten confused because of her fear and grief about Lauren.

But no matter how hard she tried to convince herself that what she felt for Nick wasn't love, but rather some combination of gratitude and friendship, she couldn't.

She knew what was in her heart, what was in her soul, and she knew it was the kind of love she'd always dreamed of, the kind that might have lasted a lifetime if given a chance to flourish.

But she was no match against a dead woman who had been perfect in every way for him. She couldn't battle the guilt that would keep Nick a victim, tied to a tragedy that would forever resonate in his soul.

She sat up straighter in her seat as a car pulled into Jimmy's driveway. She couldn't tell who was driving from the distance she was parked away from the house, but Jimmy came running out of the front door and hopped into the passenger seat.

As the car backed out of the driveway Lexie started the engine of her own vehicle. She waited until the car she intended to follow turned right on Main Street and then she put her car into gear.

Tailing somebody without discovery in a town the size of Widow Creek wasn't an easy feat. There were rarely enough cars on the road to get lost in a crowd. It would have been much easier in Kansas City where the traffic was busy.

Still, she got lucky. When she turned onto Main Street there were two cars between her and her quarry, making it easy for her to keep some distance.

It was possible they were headed to another friend's house, or just taking a drive. She told herself not to get excited, that this might just be another exercise in futility.

She slowed a bit as she lost one of the cars between them, not wanting to draw any attention to herself. Hopefully the two boys in the car weren't savvy enough to worry about anyone tailing them. Besides, the road was straight and she had no trouble keeping the vehicle in sight.

A burst of adrenaline torched through her as the car left the city limits, heading in the direction of Nick's place and Lauren's house. Where were they going?

They passed both Lauren's and Nick's houses and continued on. Then, to her stunned surprise, they turned into the lane that she knew led to Clay Cole's place.

She drove on past, her heart pounding a million beats

a minute. Clay Cole. Of course, why hadn't she and Nick thought of him?

The expensive furnishings, the plethora of toys and electronics inside his house all spoke of money to spare, money that Nick didn't think came from Clay's ranching efforts. Was it possible that the money came from selling drugs?

She found a place to ease her car off the road and parked, adrenaline spiking through her as she realized she might be getting closer to identifying the person who had killed her sister.

Once she'd parked, she pulled her cell phone from her purse.

Lexie wasn't a fool. She knew she was teetering on dangerous ground and she suddenly realized she wanted somebody to know what she was doing and where she was. The only person she knew to call was Nick.

She was aware of the fact that she'd been fairly cool to him the night before and as the phone rang a second time she hoped he wasn't avoiding her calls.

He answered on the third ring, his voice slightly breathless. "I just had the dogs out for a run," he said. "It's good to hear your voice, Lexie."

Her heart squeezed tight, but she kept focused on the reason for the call. "I just wanted somebody to know that I followed Jimmy Morano and one of his friends as they drove out of town a little while ago."

"Lexie, where are you? Where's Amberly? Is she with you?" His voice was low and vibrated with sudden tension.

"Actually she was called back to Kansas City this morning and I'm sitting in my car just down the road from Clay Cole's place. I'm parked in a grove of trees so nobody can see I'm here from the house."

"You should have called me when she left town. Get out of there, Lexie. You shouldn't be out there all alone. Come on back here to my place and we'll sort it all out here."

"Don't worry. Nobody knows I'm here and I'm not unarmed," she assured him. Her mind whirled with a million thoughts a minute. "I'm just going to sit tight for a little while and see if the boys come right out. When I get to your place we need to do a little computer research on Clay Cole's finances. We should have seen the red flags when we saw the inside of his house."

"Just get out of there," Nick exclaimed.

"I'll call you back when I'm leaving. Give me thirty minutes or so." She didn't wait for his response, but ended the call and dropped her phone back into her purse.

She wasn't about to do what he'd asked. This might be the first real break they got. She felt perfectly secure in her car with her gun in her purse next to her.

She tapped her fingers impatiently on the steering wheel, trying to decide what to do next. It was possible the boys had gone to Clay's to play some of his games, to just hang out in there where the electronics were nothing short of amazing.

She rolled down her window and tried to listen for any sounds coming from the direction of the house. If there was something screwy with Clay's finances, she'd find it. That's what she did; that was part of her expertise. She could make a computer dance and sing with personal information about somebody if she wanted.

She should have done some computer work the day that she and Nick had seen the inside of Clay's house, when they had first speculated about the source of his money. She cursed the fact that while both of them had marveled at the things he owned, neither of them had thought about checking it out further.

Was this just another wild goose chase? Was she targeting the wrong kid, chasing the wrong motive? It was possible that Clay made enough money ranching to buy his toys. It had been evident that he wasn't spending much on the maintenance of the exterior of his home.

After several more minutes passed she began to doubt what she was doing here. She wasn't about to confront Clay Cole all alone. That would be the height of foolishness. She really wasn't going to learn anything even when the kids came out of his house.

The best thing she could do now was get to her computer and do some digging into Clay Cole's life. It was time to get out of here.

She moved her hand to her keys but just before she could crank the engine the barrel of a gun pressed hard against the side of her head.

"Well, well, if it ain't the pretty pink-haired woman sticking her nose in where it don't belong." Clay's deep voice filled her with horror as she shot a glance at her purse with her gun inside.

"Whoa, if I were you I wouldn't move a muscle that I don't tell you to move. Now, nice and easy, get out of the car. If you make a wrong move I'll blow your brains out, and trust me, I'm a man of my word."

NICK PACED THE FLOOR of his living room waiting for Lexie to call and tell him she was on her way to his place. He fought the desire to jump in his car and head to Clay's, afraid if he did she'd show up here, afraid that he might miss a call from her. He didn't think she had the number to his cell. Any time she'd called him it had always been on his landline.

When twenty minutes had passed and she still hadn't shown up or called him back and he couldn't stand it any longer, he called her on her cell phone. When the call went directly to her voice mail a sick panic slithered through him.

He had no reason to believe that anything was wrong or that she was in any kind of real trouble, but he couldn't stop the alarms ringing in his head.

He was afraid to call Gary Wendall for backup. He still wasn't sure the lawman could be trusted. But as the minutes continued to click off, he recognized he had to do something. By the time forty minutes had passed and she still hadn't shown up and still wasn't answering her phone, he'd made a decision.

He grabbed his gun and was headed to the front door when he paused, his mind racing. He felt the same way he had when Danielle had told him she was leaving him…helpless and afraid that somehow he hadn't done enough.

He never wanted to feel that way again. He pulled his cell phone from his pocket and got the number to the FBI field office in Kansas City. When he connected with the office he asked to speak to Director Grimes.

"I think one of your agents is in trouble," he said when the man got on the phone. He quickly explained the situation and was glad to realize that apparently Lexie had already told her boss much of what had been happening.

"Is there law enforcement there that you can trust?" Grimes asked.

Nick hesitated only a moment. "No."

"I'll get agents there as quickly as I can," Grimes replied.

Nick gave him Clay's address. "That's where she was the last time I talked to her, but I don't intend to wait for the cavalry," he exclaimed. "I'm headed there now." He ended the call and headed out the door. He got into his truck and roared out of his driveway, recriminations firing through him.

He shouldn't have waited so long to call Grimes. He should have left for Clay's the minute she'd called and told him she was there.

He hadn't done enough.

The words thundered in his head, a repeat of what he'd heard for months after Danielle had been found dead. He'd somehow let her down, he thought, but it wasn't Danielle who filled his mind, it was Lexie.

Maybe she was fine and just hadn't answered his calls. Things had definitely gone awkward between them. Maybe she'd instantly regretted calling him in the first place and had simply left Clay's and gone back to her motel.

No, she wouldn't do that. She knew him well enough to know that he'd worry and she would never do that to him. Something was wrong, dammit.

He'd pushed her too hard, wanted her too much. That's what had run her out of his house and into danger all alone. If something happened to Lexie he didn't know if he could survive it. She was in his heart so deep that he felt that if something happened to her it would stop beating altogether.

As he got closer to Clay's place his mind began to work scenarios. He couldn't go in guns blazing; he had no idea what he might be walking into or who he might be facing.

He looked for Lexie's car when he got close to Clay's, but didn't find it parked anywhere along the road. Had she left the area? Was she maybe on his way back to his place? He frowned and dismissed the idea. She hadn't been in town long enough to know all the back roads. If she'd been on his way to his house he would have met her.

He parked his car about a mile away from Clay's house behind a grove of trees on Old Man Johnson's property. Before he left the car he pulled his cell phone from his pocket and tried one last call to Lexie's cell phone. Once again it went directly to her voice mail.

A tight tension coiled in his belly. He had no plan as he left his car. He had no idea what he intended to do, but rather moved on instinct.

This was the last place she had been and he wouldn't be satisfied until he'd checked every inch of Clay's place to assure himself that she wasn't there.

He approached Clay's house from the back, using the cover of trees to assess the situation. Unfortunately there was nothing to see. There was no sign of life anywhere.

With a frown he decided to check the outbuildings first and if he didn't find Lexie somewhere soon he'd take the chance and knock on Clay's door, insist the man show him every room in the house.

What worried him was that if she wasn't here, then he was wasting precious time. But the truth of the matter was if she wasn't here he wouldn't know where else to look.

Thankfully Clay's property was overgrown and unkempt, allowing Nick to use the cover of brush and trees to make his way to the detached garage.

His heart thundered with anxiety as he approached the building. *Lexie, where are you?* He felt the same sickening sense of danger that he'd felt when Danielle had first disappeared, the horrifying sense that something was desperately wrong.

Peering into one of the filthy garage windows, Nick's pounding heart seemed to crash to a halt. Inside, nestled next to Clay's big pickup, was Lexie's car.

Along with a renewed, nearly crippling guilt that

gripped him came a rage he'd never known before, a rage directed at Clay and whoever else was a participant in this.

Nick's fingers tightened on the butt of his gun. If he found out that Clay had hurt Lexie, Nick had no doubt that he could kill the man.

From his vantage point it looked as if Lexie's car was empty, but he needed to get inside the garage to know for sure. He crept around to the opposite side of the building and found a side door unlocked.

He slid inside, his heart once again crashing in his chest as he approached her car. The interior was empty but her keys hung from the ignition.

He stared at the trunk, afraid to open it, afraid not to. He leaned into the driver side and popped the trunk latch and then, with feet that felt like lead, he approached the trunk.

It was ajar only an inch, not enough for him to see if she was inside. Tears burned in his eyes and a lump in his throat made it almost impossible to breathe as he pulled up the trunk lid.

A gasp of relief exploded out of him. She wasn't there, but her purse was. The sight of her purse sent him into a new panic.

She was here.

And she was in desperate trouble.

Now all he had to do was find her and pray that he wasn't already too late.

Chapter Twelve

Lexie twisted and turned her wrists, attempting to break free of the rope that held her captive. Her hands were tied behind her back, and her ankles were trussed together as well, making it impossible for her to escape from the shed where Clay had stuck her.

As if the ropes that bound her weren't enough, he'd duct-taped her mouth closed as well. She was trapped, unable to scream for help and unable to help herself.

Leaning her head back against the metal structure, she fought against the tears that begged to be released, knowing that crying would solve nothing.

She'd been stupid. She should have never followed Jimmy Morano on her own. She should have never trusted that just because she was an FBI agent and carried a gun she wasn't making a huge mistake.

She'd gone off half-cocked like the Lone Ranger, her only thought trying to find somebody to blame for her sister's death. Now she had the face of at least one of the bad guys emblazoned in her brain. Clay Cole. But in identifying Cole, she'd also put herself in imminent danger.

What she hoped for was that Nick would worry when she hadn't called him again and would come looking for her. What she really hoped was that he wouldn't show up here without a plan and find himself in trouble as well.

But what frightened her more than anything was that she knew that if she didn't survive this, Nick would find a way to blame himself and she knew he'd never recover. It didn't matter that he didn't love her, she would still be, in his mind, another woman he'd somehow let down.

She squeezed her eyes closed and thought about Danielle. She had no idea exactly what had transpired between Nick and Danielle when they'd lost their baby, but there was no doubt in her mind that Nick had done everything humanly possible to support the woman he loved.

Whatever forces had driven Danielle to commit suicide, Lexie couldn't imagine that Nick had been one of them. All thoughts of Nick and Danielle jumped from her mind as she heard approaching footsteps.

The shed door creaked open and Clay walked in. He leaned against the opened door and grinned at her. "I'd ask you if you were uncomfortable, but I can tell by looking at you that you are," he said. "Unfortunately it's going to be a little while before something happens. I've got to wait for the boss man to show up and tell me exactly what he wants to do with you."

Lexie stared at him through narrowed eyes.

He laughed. "Now I understand that expression 'if

looks could kill.'" He sobered. "It's a damn shame, really. A pretty girl like you finding yourself in this mess. You should have buried your sister and hightailed it back to Kansas City. You should have never started sticking your nose in things that don't concern you."

He shoved himself off the door. "Your sister, she was going to be trouble, that's for sure. We had to arrange that little accident for her before she started training dogs that would screw up everything we're doing."

They'd killed her. Just as Lexie had suspected, they'd killed Lauren. As grief and rage exploded through her, she fought her ropes, struggling to get free so she could kill him. Sobs welled up in her throat, strangled from release by the duct tape across her mouth as the ropes held tight.

"It was the same thing with Nick's wife," he continued. Lexie froze and once again stared at him. "She had a habit of sticking her nose in where it didn't belong. She was way too curious about things for her own good."

He offered her a self-satisfied smile. "That was a piece of work if I do say so myself," he said. "The way I staged that scene so that everybody would believe she'd blown her own brains out. It was genius and it didn't hurt that she had a history of depression."

Nick. Oh, Nick, Lexie's heart cried. He'd carried the burden so long of Danielle's death and the truth was she hadn't committed suicide, but had been brutally murdered.

The next thing that chilled her blood was the knowledge that Clay had already killed two women. There was absolutely no reason to believe that she was going to suffer any different fate. Clay wasn't going to let her just walk out of this shed with the promise that she'd hightail it out of town.

A deep, shuddering chill worked through her as she realized Widow Creek wasn't just going to claim her sister's life, but her own as well.

NICK SAGGED TO THE GROUND behind the shed, over-whelmed with a myriad of emotions as he heard Clay's words. She hadn't killed herself! Danielle hadn't taken her own life. That meant she hadn't given up on them; she hadn't given up on Nick. She'd planned on getting back with him, expected to continue to build a life together.

He'd been about to check out the barn in the distance when he'd seen Clay leave the house and enter the small shed. He'd made his way to the back of it in time to hear everything that the man had said to Lexie.

Tears once again burned in his eyes, this time for the woman he'd loved, for the woman he'd believed he'd somehow let down. The tears were quickly followed by a rage like he'd never known before. They'd already stolen from him one woman he loved. He would not let them take another.

What worried him was that the whole time Clay had been talking, Lexie hadn't made a sound. Was she hurt? Was she unable to make a sound because she was in-jured? Weak?

There was only one person in there with Lexie and

Clay wouldn't be expecting Nick, especially Nick with a gun. He pulled himself up and was about to round the side of the shed when he heard a car door slam shut.

He pressed against the back of the shed so that he wouldn't be in sight of whoever was coming. The boss, that's what Clay had said. He'd been waiting for the boss to arrive.

Footsteps approached, heavy and crunching dead leaves. Gary Wendall? Was it possible the chief of police was the Mr. Big behind everything?

Nick's heart beat so furiously he found it difficult to draw a full breath. He was afraid to ease around the corner and see who was coming, afraid that he might be seen and the last hope to save Lexie would be gone.

Instead he placed his ear against the side of the shed, knowing he'd be able to hear whatever was going on inside. "Clay, take that duct tape off her mouth so we can have a civilized conversation here."

Stunned surprise filled Nick as he recognized the voice. Mayor Vincent Caldwell. So, the rot in Widow Creek had gone all the way to the top.

"You bastard, you killed my sister. You killed Nick's wife." Lexie's voice was strong and filled with emotion and the sound of it shot a rivulet of relief through Nick.

"You have become quite a nuisance, Ms. Forbes," Vincent said. "I'm trying to keep a town alive here and sometimes the individual has to be sacrificed for the good of the people."

"You're nothing more than a drug dealer," Lexie exclaimed.

"I'm doing what I have to do in order to keep this town functioning. Do you have any idea what it costs for snow removal each year? For trash pickup? Do you know what it takes to keep a town functioning? This isn't just about selling drugs, it's about our very survival here in Widow Creek."

"Is Gary Wendall one of your henchmen? Does he sell meth in his spare time?" Lexie asked.

Vincent laughed. "Gary Wendall is a lazy buffoon. Unfortunately he's a straight arrow so we've had to work around him. Fortunately for us it's been pretty easy to get around him."

Nick found some comfort in the fact that Gary hadn't been a part of Danielle's death, that he wasn't a part of the madness that had gripped this town. Still it was small comfort because Nick now had two men to get through in order to save Lexie.

"You're insane," Lexie exclaimed. "You think snow removal is worth two women's lives? You really want me to believe that you're so noble and just doing this to save the town and not lining your own pockets in the process?"

"Of course I'm lining my own pockets," Vincent said, speaking as if talking to a mentally challenged person. "But, I'm also taking care of my people…the good people of Widow Creek."

Nick wanted to burst inside. His natural instinct to protect Lexie surged up inside him. The element of surprise would be on his side, but a voice of reason reminded him that he didn't know if Clay and Vincent were armed.

Lexie could be shot in the blink of an eye and then nothing else would matter in the world. *Patience,* he told himself. He had to be patient and wait for the perfect opportunity to act. He just prayed that opportunity would come before all was lost.

LEXIE FINALLY HAD her answers. Lauren had been murdered along with Nick's wife over a year ago to protect a drug operation. The rage that filled her as she looked at Clay and Vincent nearly blinded her. Beneath the rage was a pounding terror as she recognized she was going to die here in this shed.

She had no idea where Nick was, or if he were even looking for her. Maybe he was still at his place, waiting for her to call, wondering if she would really call him.

"What about Jimmy Morano? Is he in on this?" she asked.

"He's just a stupid kid who takes care of selling to the teenagers around town. Unfortunately, he likes to use more than he likes to sell," Clay replied.

"So, it was you who shot at us at Lauren's place?" she asked Clay.

"Yeah, it was me." Clay clapped his hand on Vincent's shoulder. "The boss here, he doesn't get his hands dirty. He leaves that kind of work to me."

Vincent moved away from him, as if disliking Clay's touch. "You should have taken the warning, Ms. Forbes, and left town. Now we not only have you as a problem, but we also have Nick."

"There's no reason to hurt him," she said quickly. "He doesn't know anything. He was just helping me, but he thought I was crazy when I told him Lauren had been murdered." She couldn't stand the idea of them harming Nick. The very thought squeezed her heart so tight in her chest she could scarcely draw a breath.

"We'll figure out how to deal with Nick later," Vincent said. "In the meantime take her out to the field and kill her. Make sure you bury her body where it won't be found."

Terror thundered in Lexie's head. She wanted to beg for her life, but she knew it wouldn't do any good. Had Danielle begged for her life? Had Lauren?

"I'm going back to the office," Vincent continued. "We'll figure out what to do with her car later this evening. Call me when you're finished here."

As he left the shed a new panic seared through Lexie. "Clay, let me go," she said as tears sprang to her eyes. "I'll head back to Kansas City and you'll never hear from me again."

"Sorry, no can do." Clay grabbed the roll of duct tape and tore off a piece. "You really believe I can just let you walk out of here? I'm afraid, Ms. Pink Hair, that you need to disappear permanently."

He slapped the duct tape back over her mouth and then cut the rope that bound her ankles and yanked her to her feet. She fought the rope that still held her wrists, desperate to get free, to at least have a fighting chance to save herself, but it was no use.

"Knock it off," Clay said with irritation as she tried to body slam into him. He held her arm painfully tight and pulled her toward the door.

Clay took one step outside and halted as Nick pressed the barrel of his gun against his temple. Lexie's heart jumped with relief as Clay released his hold on her. She sidled next to Nick, her heart crashing a million beats a minute against her chest.

"What are you going to do now, big guy? Shoot me?" Clay asked derisively. "You don't have it in you."

Lexie wanted to scream at Nick not to fire, that Vincent might still be on the property and would hear the shot and she knew he was just as dangerous as Clay.

"You're right, I don't have it in me," Nick replied. He crashed the butt of the gun into the back of Clay's head and at the same time swung his fist into Clay's stomach. Clay crumbled to the ground with a moan.

Nick then turned to Lexie, his gray eyes filled with fire. "Come on, let's get the hell out of here."

He yanked the duct tape off her mouth and grabbed her elbow and then motioned across the field. "That way," he said.

She'd been in the shed long enough that the shadows of night were beginning to fall as they took off running. With her arms tied behind her back she found it difficult to run, but with the flame of survival burning bright inside, she gave it all she had.

They hadn't gone far when they heard Clay shout.

"Dammit, I should have shot him," Nick exclaimed as they hit the cover of a grove of trees.

"Where's your car?" Lexie asked between gasps as she tried to catch her breath.

"On the other side of them," he said grimly as Vincent and Clay came into view.

Lexie cursed the fact that her hands were tied behind her back, that she didn't have a gun and couldn't help Nick defend against an assault.

Clay fired, the bullet chipping bark off the tree in front of where Nick and Lexie stood. Vincent fired as well, his shot going slightly left, but Lexie knew the closer the men approached the more accurate their shots would be.

Nick answered with a shot, at the same time scanning the area for an escape route.

"We need to split up," Lexie exclaimed. "We'll have a better chance of one of us getting out of here alive."

"No!" Nick's voice was stronger, more firm than she'd ever heard it before. "No, we stay together."

"Then we'd better move," she said, "because Clay is getting closer and Vincent has disappeared." She looked behind them, worried when she realized the grove of trees that sheltered them was small and it was probable that Vincent was now attempting to come up behind them. If he succeeded, they would never make it out of this grove alive.

And she desperately wanted to live. In the days just following Lauren's death she hadn't been so sure that she could go on. In the days since she'd realized she loved Nick and would never be able to have him forever, she'd lost some of her love of life. But it was back now, screaming through her.

She wanted to survive this and she wanted Nick to survive. It didn't matter that he didn't love her as she loved him, all that mattered was that they both escaped.

Nick fired at Clay once again, forcing Clay to hit the ground. At the same time the sound of a helicopter overhead drew Lexie's attention upward.

The helicopter was the kind used by the FBI for hostage rescue. Her heart soared as she realized help had arrived. The clearing behind Clay filled with men.

"Down on the ground. Get down on the ground," the men yelled at Clay. "Hands over your head."

Harsh voices had never sounded so sweet to Lexie's ears.

"We're here," Nick called to the advancing men. He raised his hands above his head to show them his gun and to indicate he wasn't a threat.

At that moment a gun banged and Lexie gasped as her body was pierced with an excruciating pain that stole her breath. She turned toward Nick, her mouth working but no words coming out.

He smiled at her and she tried to smile back but tears blurred her vision. The raw pain inside her clawed at her. She couldn't breathe and she wondered why she couldn't take in any air. She felt herself falling…falling. The autumn leaves around her began to spin in her head, a kaleidoscope of orange and red and finally black.

Chapter Thirteen

As Lexie hit the ground, Nick screamed to the men in the field as he fell to his knees by her side. In his peripheral vision he caught a glimpse of Vincent Caldwell in the brush behind them.

Nick didn't hesitate. He pulled his gun and fired at the man. There was no satisfaction as Vincent fell, screaming as he grabbed his thigh.

Nick threw his gun to the ground as he placed a finger on Lexie's neck, seeking a pulse, praying for a pulse. The shouts of the men and the whoop of helicopter blades overhead faded to silence as Nick leaned close to Lexie and whispered fervently.

"You have to be all right, Lexie. Open your eyes and talk to me. For God's sake, just tell me you're going to be all right."

She didn't move. Her eyes didn't magically open and there was no indication that she could hear him as he pled with her to be okay. He didn't realize he was crying until a man in a SWAT uniform touched him on the shoulder. "We have to fix her," Nick said, his voice half-strangled by emotion.

"We're going to do that," the man said as he pulled Nick to his feet. "Step back and let us take care of her."

As several men with a stretcher took over, Nick looked around him in shock. The helicopter had landed in the middle of Clay's field and Clay was in custody. Several of the men had run to Vincent, who was screaming and writhing on the ground.

It was surreal…and Nick felt as if he were moving in a fog. It was only when the men tending to Lexie began to carry her out that the fog dissipated. "Where are you taking her?" he asked, his heart pounding frantically in his chest as he saw how still, how pale she looked.

"The nearest hospital," one of the men replied.

As Nick ran after them, he realized he was in love with Lexie. His love for her roared through him with a force than nearly dropped him to his knees.

Cupid had found him twice in a lifetime. Now all he had to do was pray that she survived so he could tell her that he loved her.

He was just about to his car when a man called his name. "I'm Director Grimes," the man said as he approached Nick. "And I want to thank you for calling to let us know one of our agents was in trouble."

"She's still in trouble," Nick replied around the lump of emotion that nearly clogged his throat.

Grimes nodded. "We'll be taking things over here in Widow Creek. There will be a full investigation by us, not by the locals, and we'll see to it that this place is cleaned up."

Nick didn't care about the town. He didn't give a

damn if the whole place blew up, all he cared about was getting to the hospital and finding out about Lexie.

"I've got to go," he said and without waiting another minute he got into his car and tore off toward the Widow Creek Hospital.

He knew now that Danielle hadn't committed suicide, that he hadn't let her down, but even if he hadn't known that his love for Lexie couldn't have been denied another minute.

If he'd never known about Danielle he would have taken a chance on loving Lexie, on hoping that they could build a life together.

Why hadn't he realized sooner? He'd been so mired in his past that he hadn't been able to look toward a future, and now it might be too late.

No! No, don't think that way, he told himself. *She has to be all right. She has to be!* He couldn't lose her. He refused to allow fate to take away another woman that he loved.

He screeched into the hospital parking lot and raced toward the emergency entrance. Several of the FBI agents were there, apparently also awaiting word on Lexie's condition.

"She's in surgery," one of them told Nick. "And so is Vincent Caldwell. He's having his leg repaired." He gave Nick a small smile. "Too bad you didn't aim a little higher."

"I didn't aim at all," Nick admitted. "I was blinded by rage when I realized he'd shot Lexie. I just fired at him instinctively. Was she conscious when you brought her in?"

The man shook his head. "No, she never regained consciousness." He gestured toward one of the chairs in the waiting room. "You might as well have a seat. I have a feeling it's going to be a very long night."

Nick sat in the chair, his heart heavier than it had ever been in his life. Danielle had been stolen from him and at the time he'd thought he'd never get over it, that he'd never survive.

Then Lexie had come into his life. Lexie with her warm smile and pink hair. She'd wiggled right into his heart and the idea of burying another woman that he loved nearly shattered him.

All he could do now was wait through the dark, end-less night and see if fate would once again rip love away from him.

CONSCIOUSNESS CAME LIKE a soft whisper in her ear, tug-ging her reluctantly from sweet dreams. She'd awakened several times before only to succumb to the darkness within seconds. This time consciousness remained, although she kept her eyes closed as she assessed her condition.

She was in a small amount of pain, but nothing like the pain that had ripped through her the last couple of times she'd tried to awaken.

She knew Vincent Caldwell had shot her, but she had no memory of anything after that bullet had struck. Wiggling her fingers and toes, relief swooped through her. Whatever her injuries, everything seemed to be working okay.

Without opening her eyes she knew she was in a hospital, she could tell by the smell, by the noises that came from someplace in the distance.

She'd survived. Lauren was dead, Nick was nothing more than a fantasy, but the important thing was that Lexie had survived. As soon as she was well enough she'd go back to Kansas City, immerse herself in her work and try to find some kind of happiness that was meaningful.

That's what Lauren would have wanted for her— happiness. And as a tribute to her twin she would find a way to be happy. She finally ventured a peek at her surroundings, unsurprised to find herself in a hospital bed.

Morning sunshine streamed through the windows and she was surprised by the sight of Nick slumped down in a chair, sound asleep.

Had he been there all night? Her heart ached as she gazed at him, memorizing his handsome features for when she was back in Kansas City and feeling all alone. She would remember being held in the warmth of his arms, the fire of his lips against hers and the magic of their lovemaking for a very long time to come. The memories would both warm her and fill her with sadness.

His eyes snapped open and for a moment they were filled with a soft sleepiness that made her want to lose herself in their depths.

"You're awake," he said as he sat up and raked a hand through his hair. "How are you feeling?"

"Stiff, sore and lucky to be alive," she replied. "How long have I been out of it?"

"Three days." He got out of his chair and moved to the side of her bed.

"Three days!" She stared at him, stunned by the passage of time. "What's the damage?"

"I hope you didn't like your spleen." He stood close enough to her that she could smell the scent of him, the scent that would forever haunt her with the memory of love.

"Nah, I've never been much of a spleen person," she replied.

"You were so lucky. The bullet managed to miss every vital organ and your spine. It caught a rib and deflected into the spleen but stopped there. I imagine you'll be out of here soon, but according to Director Grimes you won't be going back to work for a little while. He's put you on medical leave."

"Who called in the cavalry?" she asked.

"I did. When you weren't answering my phone calls and you hadn't called me back, I panicked. I called Director Grimes and told him he had an agent in trouble." He rocked back on his heels and gave her the smile that shot heat through her. "I guess they take that kind of thing very seriously."

"Thank goodness. So, what's happened to Clay and Vincent?"

"Vincent is in a hospital room down the hall under

armed guards. He suffered an unfortunate incident with my gun and will walk with a limp in the prison yard. The FBI and DEA have taken over the town. Clay's barn was filled with enough chemicals to make meth for the next year. Vincent was arrogant enough to keep a file on his computer that had names of mules, places they were selling and other financial information about the operation. According to your coworkers, it wasn't a huge bust, but it was a substantial one."

"And so it's over and the guilty will pay." She studied his features and her love for him pressed tight against her chest, hurting her as deeply as the bullet that had pierced through her. "At least you should feel some peace that Danielle didn't commit suicide," she said softly.

"I am relieved over that, but I'm not at peace." He took a step closer to her and reached out and touched a strand of her hair, the strand she knew was bright pink.

"I've been a fool, Lexie, a fool trapped by a ridiculous one arrow theory that got shot all to hell the moment I laid eyes on you."

His eyes glittered with a light that shone through Lexie, heating her with the whisper of possibility. But she was afraid to hope, afraid that somehow whatever he felt for her now was simply a fleeting thing that would fade with time.

"I love you, Lexie, and I don't want to let you go," he said.

His words torched joy through her, but it was a joy tempered with harsh reality. They'd both been through such an emotional wringer. Surely he was just confused about his feelings.

"Nick, I'm in love with you, but I don't think I'm the kind of woman you want in your life forever." Pain lanced through her, a pain that had nothing to do with her physical condition.

Before he could reply Gary Wendall walked into the room. "Well, it's good to see you coming around," he said to Lexie as she used the button to raise the head of her bed a little bit. "I owe the two of you a huge apology."

He jammed his hands into his pockets and frowned. "I didn't know. I didn't have a clue about the drugs. Oh, I was aware that we had a little drug issue with some of the teenagers, but I never dreamed what Clay and Vincent and some of the others were involved in anything like this. Anyway, just wanted to stop by and let you both know I'm turning in my badge. If Widow Creek survives this scandal somebody else will be in charge of law enforcement."

"Chief Wendall, I don't think either Nick or I expect your resignation," Lexie said.

He shook his head. "I don't want it any other way. I got too complacent, too lazy. The fact that there was a drug operation taking place right under my nose and I didn't smell it lets me know I need to get out. Anyway, I just wanted to apologize to you both for not taking your concerns about your loved ones more seriously."

He didn't wait for a reply, just turned quickly and

left the room. "He's not a bad man," Lexie said. "He just wasn't a good chief of police."

Tension pressed tight in her chest as she remembered the conversation they'd been having before Gary had come into the room.

"Now, where were we?" Nick asked as he approached the side of her bed again.

"I was telling you that I'm not the right woman for you," she replied, her heart beating with a heavy dread.

"And why is that?" His gaze held hers intently as he leaned closer.

"I have pink hair," she blurted out miserably.

"I know, and I'd love you if you had green hair with purple stripes," he replied.

"I spent my whole life trying to be different from Lauren and now that she's gone I don't know who I am anymore."

His eyes were a soft gray. "Allow me to introduce you to you. Lexie, you're bright and funny and sometimes when I look at you my love for you gets so tight in my chest I can hardly breathe. You're loyal and loving and I can't imagine not having you in my life."

Lexie's heart swelled at his words. She liked who she saw reflected in his eyes, and deep down she knew she *was* that woman, the woman who could love him for a lifetime, the woman who had become his second arrow.

"Oh, Nick, I wasn't expecting you," she said as happy tears burned in her eyes.

He grinned at her. "You weren't expecting a splenectomy either, but here we are."

She laughed and then sobered. "So, where do we go from here?"

"I thought maybe you'd like to recuperate at my place and then when you're well enough we'll pack up the dogs and my belongings and head to Kansas City."

She looked at him in surprise. "You'd do that for me? You'd move from here?"

"Don't you get it? I'd follow you to the ends of the earth. I'm ready to start over, Lexie, and I know how important your job is to you. I want to be your husband and I want to be the father of your children. Tell me you want that, too."

"I do. I want that, Nick." Happiness soared through her as he leaned down and gently kissed her lips.

"Then it's settled," he said as he straightened. "The nerd has found his mate."

Lexie laughed, knowing that she'd finally found the man who understood her, the man who got her quirks and found them charming. He was the man of her dreams and now he was hers. She knew their future would be filled with happiness and love and that the socks on his feet in bed would warm hers forever.

* * * * *

REQUEST YOUR FREE BOOKS!
2 FREE NOVELS PLUS 2 FREE GIFTS!

Harlequin
INTRIGUE®

BREATHTAKING ROMANTIC SUSPENSE

YES! Please send me 2 FREE Harlequin Intrigue® novels and my 2 FREE gifts (gifts are worth about $10). After receiving them, if I don't wish to receive any more books, I can return the shipping statement marked "cancel." If I don't cancel, I will receive 6 brand-new novels every month and be billed just $4.49 per book in the U.S. or $5.24 per book in Canada. That's a saving of at least 14% off the cover price! It's quite a bargain! Shipping and handling is just 50¢ per book in the U.S. and 75¢ per book in Canada.* I understand that accepting the 2 free books and gifts places me under no obligation to buy anything. I can always return a shipment and cancel at any time. Even if I never buy another book, the two free books and gifts are mine to keep forever.

182/382 HDN FEQ2

Name _____ (PLEASE PRINT)

Address _____ Apt. #

City _____ State/Prov. _____ Zip/Postal Code

Signature (if under 18, a parent or guardian must sign)

Mail to the **Reader Service:**
IN U.S.A.: P.O. Box 1867, Buffalo, NY 14240-1867
IN CANADA: P.O. Box 609, Fort Erie, Ontario L2A 5X3
Not valid for current subscribers to Harlequin Intrigue books.

**Are you a subscriber to Harlequin Intrigue books
and want to receive the larger-print edition?
Call 1-800-873-8635 or visit www.ReaderService.com.**

* Terms and prices subject to change without notice. Prices do not include applicable taxes. Sales tax applicable in N.Y. Canadian residents will be charged applicable taxes. Offer not valid in Quebec. This offer is limited to one order per household. All orders subject to credit approval. Credit or debit balances in a customer's account(s) may be offset by any other outstanding balance owed by or to the customer. Please allow 4 to 6 weeks for delivery. Offer available while quantities last.

Your Privacy—The Reader Service is committed to protecting your privacy. Our Privacy Policy is available online at www.ReaderService.com or upon request from the Reader Service.

We make a portion of our mailing list available to reputable third parties that offer products we believe may interest you. If you prefer that we not exchange your name with third parties, or if you wish to clarify or modify your communication preferences, please visit us at www.ReaderService.com/consumerschoice or write to us at Reader Service Preference Service, P.O. Box 9062, Buffalo, NY 14269. Include your complete name and address.

HI11B

*Harlequin Romantic Suspense presents the latest book
in the scorching new* KELLEY LEGACY *miniseries
from best-loved veteran series author Carla Cassidy*

*Scandal is the name of the game as the Kelley family fights
to preserve their legacy, their hearts...and their lives.*

Read on for an excerpt from the fourth title
RANCHER UNDER COVER

*Available October 2011
from Harlequin Romantic Suspense*

"**W**ould you like a drink?" Caitlin asked as she walked to the minibar in the corner of the room. She felt as if she needed to chug a beer or two for courage.

"No, thanks. I'm not much of a drinking man," he replied.

She raised an eyebrow and looked at him curiously as she poured herself a glass of wine. "A ranch hand who doesn't enjoy a drink? I think maybe that's a first."

He smiled easily. "There was a six-month period in my life when I drank too much. I pulled myself out of the bottom of a bottle a little over seven years ago and I've never looked back."

"That's admirable, to know you have a problem and then fix it."

Those broad shoulders of his moved up and down in an easy shrug. "I don't know how admirable it was, all I knew at the time was that I had a choice to make between living and dying and I decided living was definitely more appealing."

She wanted to ask him what had happened preceding that six-month period that had plunged him into the bottom of the bottle, but she didn't want to know too much about him. Personal information might produce a false sense of intimacy that she didn't need, didn't want in her life.

"Please, sit down," she said, and gestured him to the table. She had never felt so on edge, so awkward in her life.

"After you," he replied.

She was aware of his gaze intensely focused on her as she rounded the table and sat in the chair, and she wanted to tell him to stop looking at her as if she were a delectable dessert he intended to savor later.

Watch Caitlin and Rhett's sensual saga unfold amidst the shocking, ripped-from-the-headlines drama of the Kelley Legacy miniseries in

RANCHER UNDER COVER

Available October 2011 only from Harlequin Romantic Suspense, wherever books are sold.